C000065740

VOTIVUS
REVERIE

Kayla Butler

Crystal Occult Publishing

This is a fictional work based on the mythology of various types of fae folklore. All rights reserved. Printed in the United States of America. No portion of this book may be reproduced in any whole or part, stored in a retrieval system, or transmitted in any form by any means—electronic, mechanical, photocopy, recording, scanning or other (except for brief quotations, critical review, or articles)—without the prior written permission of the publisher.

VOTIVUS REVERIE Copyright 2024 by Kayla Butler ©

Crystal Occult Publishing, Bedford, OH.

Crystal Occult Publishing books may be purchased for educational, business, or sales promotional use. For information, please email the *kbut2015@gmail.com*

Editor: *Stacey M. Robinson / KYA Publishing Canada*
Cover Design: *Chinedu Anthony (Nigeria)*
Typeset: *Ashley Mae Pancho (Philippines) /*
Ebook Design: *Osamu Diamenabdul (Nigeria)*
Contributions by *ElevatedWaves Publishing Corp. (United States)*

ISBN (Paperback): <u>979-8-9906379-0-0</u>
ISBN (E-book): <u>979-8-9906379-1-7</u>

Library of Congress Control Number (LCCN): 2024909994

This book may be purchased in bulk for educational, business, or sales promotional use via kbut2015@gmail.com

—For Taco Bell quesadillas
Absolutely delicious.

Table of Contents

CHAPTER 1 4

CHAPTER 2 12

CHAPTER 3 18

CHAPTER 4 24

CHAPTER 5 29

CHAPTER 6 34

CHAPTER 7 42

CHAPTER 8 50

CHAPTER 9 58

CHAPTER 10 67

CHAPTER 11 74

CHAPTER 12 80

CHAPTER 13 88

CHAPTER 14 96

CHAPTER 15 103

CHAPTER 16 109

CHAPTER 17 116

ABOUT THE AUTHOR 124

ACKNOWLEDGMENT 125

GLOSSARY 127

CHAPTER 1

"To those who can hear, but can not peer beyond their Veil, the howls of mystic creatures is simply that of legends. Yet for those who can take a peek, and evermore than a simple one, such creatures do exist. Their existence blots the land of humans with destruction and pain. We now understand that Pain is not a legend. Pain is real. And for humans, if one can feel pain; if one can see pain, then it must be dealt with. Do not let the Veil blind you from Pain. Bear it and look upon its disturbing howls, for sight and sound become one once the Veil is involved. Nevermore may the spirits of blight rise. Nevermore may they inflict harm on loved ones. Nevermore shall Pain reside on this side of the Veil."

— Beyond the Veil by Marcus Revenali

E ven with the notoriety of his speech, the statue had not been well cared for. It was now reduced to cracked marble, covered in moss and short vines. One of the few remaining pieces of an ancient land, that of which had now morphed into a bustling metropolis in a modern world. Yet this metropolis couldn't have gotten here without his efforts. At the heart of his city, smeared by the elements, he still vaguely glimmered under the sun. Lacuna always found herself disappointed looking at the stone's state of neglect. However, the small platelet set in the middle of its cracked pedestal had not been forgotten, and never would be, still pristine against the deteriorating marble.

"Honestly, how could people treat him this way?"

Even the Oracle's constant inquiries on near useless miscellaneous topics didn't make Lacuna this disappointed. Still, unlike how she behaved in their presence, the unkept brilliance of the decaying stone swayed her heart for a moment. Right now, Lacuna stood reverently before the moss-covered statue of Marcus Revenali, the founder and first Arius of a country that shares his name in honor.

She picked a small amount of moss from the statue and examined it in her palm before attempting to mold it into a ball.

Only residents of Revenali like herself refer to the island-like country as such. To the average person, Revenali didn't exist. It was completely unknown to the outside world: a land purposefully hidden by both natural and unnatural obstacles.

Not much was known about Marcus beyond his creation of Revenali, especially not to Lacuna. His exact appearance, specific magical abilities, or even possible family were all completely unknown. The statue and his teachings were a few of the only concepts to remember him by. That being said, there was one important piece of information that was well known about Marcus Revenali: his extreme hatred for the *fae*, the mystic creatures of this world.

Exactly as it was stated in the speech carved into his statue, *pain* is what Marcus came to solely know the *fae* as. However, these magic beings had other names as well. Some refer to them as neighbors or spirits from the Otherside, fairies of Alfheim, beings of the Wilds, and various additional terms based on region and culture.

The fae had a great amount of influence on the land of humans, their powers painfully affecting the minds and bodies of many, even when they couldn't be sensed. The Veil hid their presence and gave them shelter. It provided them with the ability to seamlessly travel between the realms in a way that humans could not. And despite feeling the brunt of all their chaos and compulsions for centuries, so much was still unknown about them.

Lacuna looked past the statue at Revenali's town square. She watched as people went by, buying food and trinkets from pale, sandy brick buildings. Old ladies talked. Children ran around and played together. Adults tended to their various duties. And no matter who they were or what they did within this island society, almost everyone in the town square, nearly everyone on the island, had a knife attached to their hip or a sword strapped to their back. Adult or child, man or woman, tall or short.

Every single person.

The fae brought so much pain to the world—Marcus' world—so after many trials and tribulations in his ancient world, Marcus Revenali made a decision. He took his mysterious powers to an island in the middle of the Bermuda Triangle, and concluded that it would be the best place to train warriors against the unknown. He collected disciples, taught them his ways, and built an entire society from the ground up.

This is how Revenali came to be. A hidden island full of faerie killers, known as Arius.

Revenali isn't the only area of the world that knows about the faerie realm. In fact, the world has become somewhat more familiar with the fae as time goes on. Their mystical presence exists all around humans, after all. And although there has never been a witch alive that was as powerful as Marcus Revenali, witches in general have become much more accepted in the modern world in subtle ways.

Lacuna spotted a poster on the wall of a small cafe:

Have you spotted a witch? Report the sight to the Runic Arius.
Bounty: 500 RD per witch caught. Call #: (XXX)-XXX-XXXX

Although, this evidently didn't apply in Revenali. Witches were allies of fae who encouraged their way of life, while Arius were warriors that fought against their wickedness. Warriors who would follow in the footsteps of Marcus Revenali.

Lacuna was finally one of these warriors now. She'd waited eighteen years to do so.

Early fall settled in Revenali, although autumn's signature colors were nowhere in sight. As per usual, the trees remained the same all year round. A cold breeze blew; gently moving through Lacuna's dark coily hair. She shivered, not only due to the breeze, but with excitement too. Lacuna normally didn't become excited. Not even the rare instances in which the Oracle giving her chocolate after training could do that. Yet, today was different.

Her first official mission would be assigned soon.

Lacuna stopped playing with the moss in her hand, letting the small sphere she made fall to the ground silently. She looked upon the statue a final time with an unusual sense of hope and enthusiasm.

Lacuna was feeling a lot of strong emotions today. Taking a deep breath, she checked her phone, noting that it was 2:38 P.M. She then turned on her heels and walked towards Altare Mountain, home of Oracle's Temple, and where she lived as well.

As long as the Oracle didn't sense her level of excitement once she arrived, she would be fine.

While other Arius would hone their skills at an official academy in Revenali, Lacuna was personally taught by the one and only Oracle of the country. Over the years, she realized that this Oracle title did not refer to any actual ability to tell the future, such as what oracles in most fairy tales and myths did. It instead referred to the way that the Oracle could somewhat mold one's future to their will. Within their presence, it was as if life itself were the moss ball Lacuna was fiddling with mere moments ago. People often followed the Oracle's wishes subconsciously once met by their masked but piercing gaze.

In a way that was somewhat similar to Marcus Revenali, nothing was known about the Oracle. Not even fundamental parts of their identity. Their appearance was hidden behind heavy robes and a light blue, corvid-like mask. They possessed a voice that was low, but smooth and unwavering with no real bass behind it. Not even Lacuna could figure out who the Oracle truly was, even despite being taught and raised by the Oracle themself and their associates. Too mysterious. In Lacuna's mind they were just *the Oracle* instead of a *person*. But they were evidently human.

At the base of Altare mountain was a staircase. Built by the original disciples of Marcus, the ancient piece of architecture swept across the entire mountain range. The main landing was barely visible from the bottom of the mountain's stairway. After scaling the staircase, Lacuna had arrived at the doors of the temple. She checked her phone one more time. It was now 2:59 P.M.

"Just in time," Lacuna thought to herself.

After putting her phone away, she pushed against the temple's pearlescent double doors and walked inside. She then headed towards the Oracle's office, after a short climb up another set of stars. Even with how expansive the temple was, the office wasn't far from the main entrance. One would only need to make a simple turn to arrive at the Oracle's office once upstairs. The direction of this turn, of course, also depended on the staircase taken, as there were three in the rather wide-looking foyer. Lacuna simply took the main staircase, which also happened to be the largest and most straightforward of all three. No turning was needed.

Simple—exactly as she liked it.

Many citizens of Revenali often theorized that the Oracle may not be human, yet there had never been much evidence to support such claims. Even still, Lacuna sometimes found herself agreeing with these theories, despite knowing better.

Soon, Lacuna arrived at the doorway to the Oracle's office. Its own double doors were similar to the entrance of the temple itself. In a way, these doors were even more grand than the ones outside. And luckily, they were already open.

As she stepped inside, the Oracle had their back turned to her from a few meters away, humming an incoherent tune while searching through a nearby bookshelf behind their desk. Lacuna swore that, sometimes, her mysterious caretaker truly did appear to be faintly glowing. Yet it was possibly due to the large windows which encompassed their entire office, sunlight flowing in and reflecting off their satin robes. Lacuna took note of this instead of using the sight to further speculate on the Oracle's humanity. It probably wouldn't be wise to do such a thing in their presence anyway. Sometimes, it was as if they could hear her thoughts.

Coincidently, they acknowledged her presence without turning to look at her. "You know, I was beginning to worry, Lacuna. It would have been very disappointing if you were late for your first mission." They paused, focusing on one book in particular. "However, it appears that you are right on time."

The Oracle picked the book off the shelf and began flipping through it. Their voice carried the same impassive tone as they mumbled, "Excellent."

For a moment, Lacuna wasn't sure if the Oracle was referring to their book selection or her timing. Perhaps it was both.

They had a habit of not looking at Lacuna when speaking to her. She couldn't tell why they did it, unable to get a clue even after so many years living with them. But no matter how often the question entered her mind, she knew that it could never be asked out loud. Such questions didn't matter much anyway. No one questions how the Oracle operates.

"Of course, Your Highness," Lacuna replied with a leveled voice.

Respect was crucial within the presence of the Oracle. Even in comparison to the current leader of Revanali, Morana Rune, the Oracle was essentially a monarch. They had an authority that could only be bestowed by deities. Or near deities, like Marcus.

"So Lacuna, are you ready to finally know your mission?" The Oracle finally looked up at her, still impassive. They sat down, light from the large office windows falling over an emotionless mask.

"Yes, Your Highness."

"Excellent," they said a second time. "Here's what you need to know."

The Oracle then grabbed the book they were previously flipping through and turned it around to show Lacuna its contents. Within the visible page was an illustration of a faerie, but not just any faerie. A Feomin: one of the most powerful creatures of the Faerie Court outside its monarch. Just as it was illustrated in the Oracle's book, such fae usually had long dark hair that contrasted with sharp white teeth. It possessed equally darkened scleras which laid behind blood-red irises. Elvish ears and languid black tails twitched constantly with what Lacuna considered to be absolutely repulsive creepiness. Its nearly vanta-black hands faded into a dark gradient, and their wickedness was further emphasized by sharp, similarly black nails. Looking at the image was like looking at a depiction of a biblical devil.

At least when thinking of other fae, a somewhat angelic, fairy-like image comes to the mind of most. It was agreed that Feomin, however, were absolutely demonic pests. But unlike flies, they weren't easy to get rid of and they didn't die in just five days. As Lacuna stood off-put by the image for a few seconds, the Oracle spoke again.

"One of these has been spotted by a Revenalian scout stationed in America. Your mission will be to get rid of it. Your target was located in the town of Podim, Ohio. It's masquerading as a human college student. Supposedly, it's been attending a school known as Podim University for a year. It's referred to by others as Sonai Adalim. Based on these images..."

The Oracle then put down the book and picked up a tablet instead. They showed it to Lacuna. It displayed an actual photo of a Feomin rather than a drawn illustration. Lacuna found this even more off-putting. She felt a strange feeling swirl in her stomach. The Oracle then swiped to the right and an image of a human-looking girl was shown. But she obviously wasn't human. It was simply the human form that Lacuna's Feomin was using. Most fae had the power to take on a human-like appearance after crossing the Veil. Witches and Arius alike have referred to this power as Glamour. And Lacuna could admit that based on the picture, it was a pretty seamless transformation. Not a single inhuman feature in sight. Lacuna even found her somewhat pretty.

"... it is a female with curly black hair, brown skin, and brown eyes, as you can see. Should be around five feet and eight inches tall. Possesses immense powers as expected. According to a few scouts, they appear to be fire based, so watch out for burns." Lacuna could feel the Oracle look straight into her eyes as they asked, "Do I need to repeat any of the previous information?"

"No, Your Highness."

"Excellect." The tablet was turned off. "Assuming that you've looked at the messages I've been sending you for the past week, you have now been enrolled at Podim University. You must track down the Feomin and assassinate her without alerting any non-Revenalian citizens. Which will be a lot, based on the location. I advise you to take as much time as you need since your enemy is very powerful. Our research thus far has concluded that Feomin are a level five threat, possibly nearing guardian levels in terms of magical ability and mystic energy. Take note of this and proceed with caution. They're able to stay within the human side of the Veil for as long as they wish, due to these powers." The Oracle's tone was low with warning. "You must be careful, Lacuna. Extremely careful. Now, do you understand everything I have explained?"

"Yes, Your Highness." Lacuna repeated for a third time. "You have tasked me with the mission of taking down a female Feomin in Podim, Ohio. I have as much time as needed to complete the mission since I should be as careful as possible."

Lacuna stated this calmly. But she wasn't really calm, despite how hard she was trying to be. Her first official mission was going to involve taking down a Feomin! In fact, the Oracle's request didn't make any sense. This seemed more like the type of mission that an Arius like Morana Rune would be tasked with, not Lacuna.

And once again, as if they could read her thoughts, the Oracle inquired, "You're probably wondering why I have given you this specific mission." It was more of a statement than a question. They stood up from their chair and glided towards Lacuna, placing a cold gloved hand on her shoulder. "I do not doubt your abilities in any way, Lacuna. In truth, I believe that you are one of Revenali's strongest soldiers. I made sure of that. I plan to use this mission to test you."

The Oracle's tone momentarily shifted into something more caring than their previous impassiveness. "If you can complete it successfully, not only will you bring another sliver of peace into the human realm, but I will also have you join the Runic Arius as an honorary reward."

Ever since she was a child, it had been her dream to become an outstanding Arius. One like Marcus Revenali or the nation's current leader Morana. And the greatest Arius of all time were those who were in the battle units of Revenali's leaders. Not only would it be an absolute honor to join Morana Rune, but there was also a tradition in Revenali which involved the title of the country's greatest Arius unit being based on the last name of its leader. To Lacuna, essentially taking up the leader's last name for Arius activities was like getting adopted into a family.

She'd always wanted one of those.

With a quick nod, Lacuna replied, "I see, Your Highness. Thank you for this opportunity."

The Oracle nodded back. "Now Lacuna, pack your bags and make your way to Revenali's eastern portal gate. Runic Arius Jordan Mitchels will meet you there to send you off on your mission. I have requested that you enter Podim, Ohio by 4:30 P.M. and arrive at the Podim University campus by 5:00 P.M. Right now it is 3:30. You have exactly one hour."

With that, Lacuna gave the Oracle a final thankful nod and left the office. She proceeded to make her way towards her own bedroom. As she walked, Lacuna traced her finger against the grooves of the temple's white walls. She lived within these walls for as long as she could remember. Although, it had been even longer than that, according to the Oracle. Eighteen years ago, a random woman had dropped her at the temple doorstep. And no matter how hard the temple workers tried to locate the woman, they couldn't find her. She had no data within Revenali's database. Less than four thousand people lived in Revenali; she shouldn't have been hard to find.

Lacuna recalled when the Oracle explained to her that the woman likely wasn't from Revenali.

"Her arrival and disappearance is one of the country's biggest mysteries," they chuckled.

Remembering the way they laughed at their own comment highlighted the oddity of her situation. The Oracle didn't laugh often. And it wasn't funny to Lacuna in any capacity.

Why did her mother want to make sure no one could find her? What reason did she have to send her unwanted child to a hidden island? Why didn't she just get rid of her?

Did she really hate her that much?

Lacuna picked up a large plain backpack sitting in the corner of her room. She grabbed multiple sets of clothing, hygienic items, cash, and other essential objects for her soon-to-be college life. This included her high tech retractable swords, which she attached to her belt with a *click*.

Lacuna looked around her room a final time, but it wasn't like there was much to look at. The room was extremely plain: a bed with white sheets, but without a headboard. A cream colored nightstand with an alarm clock. A similarly colored dresser, now emptied of all its clothing. A small bookshelf that had no real use. And the temple had its own, much more expansive library anyway. There was a single book on the shelf. It was titled *Eternal Wood*.

The book detailed the story of a girl searching for her lost mother in a dangerous forest full of mystic creatures. Eventually she learns that her mother has been turned into a creature herself. Maybe if Lacuna's mother had been turned into a faerie, her actions would make more sense. But she couldn't be, since Lacuna was fully human.

Lacuna stared blankly at the shelf for a few seconds.

She walked towards the bookshelf and placed the novel into her bag. Now she was ready to go.

At 4:00 P.M, Lacuna had finally arrived at Revenali's eastern portal gate. She could see the ocean clearly from here. The ground was covered in a glittery, pale lavender stone. Various thick pillars of a similar color were scattered around the area. They were gargantuan in height, appearing as though they were endlessly reaching into the sky. After gazing upon the pillars, Lacuna continued to look down at the rest of the area. A substantial mass of Arius were located within the area. Dozens were sent out daily through Revenali's portal gate system, since the magical gates were one of the only ways to access the outside world. That is, unless a person came by ship. But that would be too dangerous. Even while ignoring the island country's extreme oceanic location, it was also surrounded by a magic barrier. Only powerful magic users could see Revenali from the outside.

And yet, there were still docks stationed near certain portal gates, such as this one. A gentle breeze blew, carrying saltwater-scented air through the area; the journeys of travelers and their long forgotten tales passed through her mind along with the air. As she thought of ships, Lacuna looked towards the ocean.

"Lacuna Cryoni?" asked an unknown voice.

"Hmm? Yes, I am the person you're searching for." Lacuna turned around.

Standing a couple feet behind her was a young man, most likely around her age, yet possibly a little bit older. His appearance was—striking—to say the least. He was wearing a black tuxedo and maroon dress pants with deep pockets. Their depth was very apparent to Lacuna due to how far his hands were inside of them. His hair, a similar texture to her own, was combed over his forehead, yet curled upwards to the left. He wore glasses with thin golden frames. A small chain of a similar color was attached to the frames near his right eye. However, the most striking thing about the man's appearance was his earrings. The one on his right ear was a gold stud while the one on his left was a long golden dangle. The chain of his glasses was connected to the stud earring.

"Nice to meet you. I'm Jordan Mitchels and I will be your main advisor during your mission." He held out his right hand; his left one stayed in his pocket.

Lacuna shook his hand gently as she replied, "Hello, Sir Mitchels."

"Just Jordan is fine."

Lacuna nodded. Jordan led the two of them towards one of the many pillars in the area. It had a strange symbol carved into it.

"Does this one lead to Ohio?" asked Lacuna.

"Yes." Jordan then took his hand out of his left pocket. He was holding a small crystal with an interesting shape. The shape matched perfectly with the carving on the pillar.

He placed the crystal inside the pillar's carving. It began to glow violently. As the light grew, Jordan closed his eyes.

"You may want to turn your eyes away for a second, Lacuna."

Lacuna turned away as Jordan recommended. Just in time too. The light had become so bright that Lacuna could see it from underneath her eyelids. Soon after, the bright light was replaced by a more gentle glow. The entire pillar had become a portal.

"Are you ready?"

Lacuna nodded. She held onto the straps of her backpack tightly. She had never used a portal before, but there was no time to be nervous. A Feomin was up to who knows what within the human realm and it was up to Lacuna to stop her. So she walked into the glowing pillar and let its unknown light carry her body away from the ocean, warriors, and empty temples.

Towards the future.

CHAPTER 2

L acuna didn't know what to expect when she arrived in Podim, Ohio. But it definitely wasn't this.

She and Jordan were currently standing in an alleyway. The area was sandwiched between an abandoned coffee shop and a small shoe store. Both buildings were made from a gray cobblestone, and their exterior walls, at least the ones visible in the alley, were caked with dirt. Cigarette butts and a few plastic coffee cups were littered across the area. While she wasn't hoping to end up anywhere in particular, objectively, this wasn't somewhere that most would expect the end of a magic portal to lead. Initially, it was more likely that they'd end up in a forest, or a building owned by Revenali. Or at the very least, the college she's supposed to be stationed at. Instead, Lacuna's first experience in Ohio only allowed her to tell why the coffee shop closed down.

Base color of the cups: white. A background for the large green circle that surrounded a small dog in the shape of a coffee bean. The dog's eyes were so large that they not only took up half the cup, but also escaped the circle that the rest of its body was in. The final nail in this horrendously designed coffin was the company name, the words *Cane Corso Coffee* written around the circle. Appearing more like a bug than a dog, Lacuna also found it odd that the mascot was a Cane Corso of all dogs. The designers had to purposefully go out of their way to make the dog appear small despite being a depiction of a large breed. Lacuna wondered, "Did they really choose the design simply to match the pun?"

Yet worst of all was simply the way in which the dog appeared to eye her. Like it was following her movements. As if it had been patiently waiting for someone to exit the portal from the beginning.

"Podim State University is around a five minute walk from here. Simply go right and continue walking until you see it. Here's your student ID and documents," Jordan said.

She had a mission to do, and couldn't afford to get distracted by idiotic coffee cup designs. "Thank you sir." She slowly made her way out of the alley as he began reopening the portal.

From this point on, Jordan wouldn't be following her. He had his own missions to attend to. They would only meet up again once per month for progress checks.

Having the ability to take as much time as needed and knowing that the check-ins would be monthly made Lacuna nervous. She understood that the Feomin would be powerful, but what was it about her that could cause the mission to take such a long time?

She remained calm nonetheless and continued walking. As she passed civilians and observed their attire, it was evident that most of the people in the area were college students. Many around her age. There were tons of small shops on the street, all in better shape than the ridiculous coffee shop. Leaves were changing color and people scrambled around the sidewalks in sweaters. Autumn had arrived in Podim too, but the air was more mild than it was in Revenali. There was no ocean nearby.

It was quite the change of scenery.

A large flock of birds flew far overhead, their caws announcing to the world that they were a murder of crows. Eight in total, flapping far and fast, as if they too had somewhere important to be. Lacuna watched the birds with caution, until they were completely out of sight. Even despite having no real reason to fear their presence, Lacuna felt the need to be extra diligent. No matter how immersed she was in the sights of Podim, something felt *off* once she left the portal.

After walking for a few more minutes, her fear subsided slightly. And soon after, Lacuna finally spotted her destination: Podim University.

Dozens of students were filtering in and out of the gate that separated the rest of the city from the monumental college building. The sidewalks and the rest of the property were a mixture of white, tan and scarlet red brick. It was a gorgeous sight in contrast with the falling leaves of autumn. Lacuna had never experienced a sight like it before. Even though the seasons changed just the same in Revenali, the leaves never changed colors to signify it. She could only ever tell by the wind.

Lacuna continued her walk through the gates, pushing past fellow college students. She began to ponder once again regarding her current situation. How was the American education system in comparison to Revenali's? Or rather, not even Revenali's. She never received an official Revenalian education, as she was technically home-schooled by the Oracle. Thus the real question was, how did her Oracle-led education different from both? Lacuna really was going to be attending college like all the people around her now. But for how long? This was all simply a part of an elaborate, dangerous mission after all.

The thought left her contemplating the Oracle's choice. Her current knowledge of fae spanned only from the pages of books. She had no sense of field experience or knowledge of specific tricks and tactics used by fae in battle. All she knew was that they were tricky and their rules didn't often follow common sense.

Absorbed by the thought of such trickery, Lacuna's shoulder bumped into someone. A bundle of books, papers, and various art supplies came tumbling to the ground.

"Sorry," Lacuna exclaimed impassively, picking up the mess she caused.

A meek voice replied, "It's alright," as she hurriedly picked up her items.

The girl that Lacuna had just run into was covering her face with the hood of a large, light blue hoodie. As she reached down to grab another book, long hair–seemingly dyed from a purple to light blue gradient–fell from her hood like a waterfall. The color reminded Lacuna of gems like sapphire or tanzanite. As she stood back up again, the gemstone-haired woman readjusted her hood, just barely allowing Lacuna to see her face. A final book still laid on the ground. As Lacuna picked it up, she realized it had a very familiar title.

"Eternal Wood?" Lacuna remarked aloud.

"Um… yes. I recently started reading it," the girl replied, her tone more confident. "How about you?"

Lacuna simply looked at her blankly for a moment. The girl looked back, expecting an answer.

Lacuna simply stated, "I see," as she handed the girl the book. She then proceeded to walk away, saying nothing else.

The girl could only look back at her with a mystified expression.

Using the map and information that Jordan gave her, Lacuna eventually arrived at the Student Resource Center in high spirits. Her conversation with a senior student working at the university was relatively short, just like it was with the other girl. However, it was much more productive for Lacuna, allowing her to confirm that everything she needed was in order.

Long before this mission, the Oracle had set up a fake college application for her, complete with a false highschool transcript from, what was ironically, a real school that existed in a city far from Podim, Ohio. Events such as this happened every day for the Arius of Revenali. They had allies from all over the world, in all fields of life.

She looked at the dorm room number that was assigned to her: *235 C.*

She eventually found her destination. Just before the doors, various chimes rang in a melodic rhyme, matching perfectly with the natural chorus of the wind. If Lacuna strained her ears closely enough, all of the sounds together sounded almost like the shrill laughter of a group of children. Once again, a sense of nervousness settled in her, just like crows caws did several minutes before. Upon entering the building, Lacuna glanced at the dormitory's windows, observing how they created irregular spots of sunlight within the long, and currently empty, halls. The area was quiet. Too quiet for a college dormitory in the late afternoon.

There wasn't a window in front of room 235 C. None of the sunset's rays shined their light on Lacuna. Right as she took out her room keycard, Lacuna saw *something, someone,* out of the corner of her eye, illuminated by the sun instead. Time seemed to slow down as she turned her attention towards the unknown entity standing a few yards away.

The sight made her heart skip a beat.

The sunset filtering through the windows doused mahogany skin into a dusty amber. Long, curly raven hair cascaded towards where the light pooled onto the floor, shimmering just the same. The light reflected fires into the deep, dark brown eyes of a demon; the lids crinkled slightly as the entity grinned at her with pearlescent teeth, that of which were simply not yet fangs.

Lacuna detached one of her swords from her hip immediately. The entity currently within her presence was Sonai Adalim. Her target.

"Are you having trouble opening that door, Arius?" taunted Sonai with a chuckle. The empty hallway made her voice echo slightly. She leaned forward, tilting her head to get a better look at the door, rather than at Lacuna. Her opponent.

Somehow, Sonai already knew Lacuna was coming for her, strangely making the decision to bring the battle right to her. Whether or not Lacuna should find that worrisome didn't matter much now. Alongside the danger, it was convenient, just how she liked it.

Magic energy accumulated in the hand of the faerie as the human unsheathed her blade; both weapons shimmered like the currently setting sun. The wispy, semi-transparent red orb Sonai made was chucked at Lacuna after a second. As she did so, one foot was raised off the ground like a baseball pitcher. The motion was oddly light, and appeared to lack force. Lacuna dodged the orb, letting it hit the wall a couple feet behind her. A burnt mark was left on it instead of her.

Lacuna detached one of her swords from her hip immediately. The entity currently within her presence was Sonai Adalim. Her target.

"Are you having trouble opening that door, Arius?" taunted Sonai with a chuckle. The empty hallway made her voice echo slightly. She leaned forward, tilting her head to get a better look at the door, rather than at Lacuna. Her opponent.

Somehow, Sonai already knew Lacuna was coming for her, strangely making the decision to bring the battle right to her. Whether or not Lacuna should find that worrisome didn't matter much now. Alongside the danger, it was convenient, just how she liked it.

Magic energy accumulated in the hand of the faerie as the human unsheathed her blade; both weapons shimmered like the currently setting sun. The wispy, semi-transparent red orb Sonai made was chucked at Lacuna after a second. As she did so, one foot was raised off the ground like a baseball pitcher. The motion was oddly light, and appeared to lack force. Lacuna dodged the orb, letting it hit the wall a couple feet behind her. A burnt mark was left on it instead of her.

"Are you trying to burn the building down?" exclaimed Lacuna as she looked back at her in false shock. She already expected such dangerous behavior from a Feomin, but she wondered if the faerie would feel guilty.

"Of course not! I would never!" retorted Sonai in a quieter voice. "And shut up! Are you trying to let the entire dormitory know we're fighting up here?"

"You are the one attempting to attack me in a public building."

"You came here to try and kill me!"

"How do you know that?"

"You. Are. Holding. A. Sword." Sonai replied, emphasizing each word. "What type of person, who doesn't kill people, holds a sword?"

"I don't kill people. I eliminate dangers to the human world like you," Lacuna stated calmly. She firmly grasped the hilt and upper middle section of her sword, careful not to let her hand slide at all. Swiftly, Lacuna cracked her sword like a glowstick, transforming it into a boomerang. She threw it at Sonai with more grace than Sonai did when throwing her orb.

Sonai crouched underneath the boomerang's path, staying down for a few seconds longer to avoid getting hit when it came back around.

"You nearly took my head off!" Sonai shouted in a whiny voice when she got back up.

"Soon, I actually will," stated Lacuna calmly as she caught the boomerang. "That was a test shot. I won't miss next time."

"Eww! That'll get my blood everywhere..."

"Faeries do not bleed, they fade away after death."

"Who told you that? Some of us do, actually."

Sonai created another orb in her hand and threw it at Lacuna. Yet this one was much quicker than the last. Unsure if she could dodge it successfully or not, Lacuna opted to create a shield.

Magic energy quickly swirled towards the middle of her body, bursting out in front of her as a light, semi-transparent shield. Sonai's orb was reflected off the shield back at her, but because it was her magic originally, she simply grabbed the orb to reabsorb it. Lacuna was disappointed, although it didn't show on her face.

Sonai, however, was flabbergasted. "You just used magic!"

"Yes? That isn't unusual."

"Humans can't use magic!"

"Many Arius from Revenali can, in fact, use magic."

"The Arius that I'm familiar with," Sonai's voice was calmer than it had been throughout the entire, very short battle, "can only use weapons with powers harvested from fae they've defeated in battle." She looked at Lacuna with genuine confusion. "You just made a shield out of pure magic energy."

The fire in Sonai's eyes seemed to die down a bit, yet, it never fully went away. Her nails, which Lacuna just noticed were *very long* before, began to grow smaller. Now she had normal human nails rather than the claws they would've turned into if she transformed fully.

"This complicates things…" Sonai muttered, folding her arms. She began thinking instead of focusing on the battle.

Lacuna wondered, "What's complicated about using magic?" For the few minutes she'd known Sonai, Lacuna came to a decision.

Sonai Adalim was incredibly annoying. And stupid. Like the *Cane Corso Coffee* mascot.

All she seemed to do was complain and talk *at* her the entire battle. And she was barely putting in any effort to defend herself. What type of Feomin was she? It was about time for Lacuna to end this ridiculous fight. She doubted that the unlimited amount of time the Oracle granted her wouldn't be needed at all. Trying to fight a fae that genuinely worries about burning down buildings or being heard while in a human form? Laughable.

Lacuna cracked her sword again, changing it back into its basic state. She prepared to lunge at Sonai, and pierce her heart with it. Sonai, the so-called dangerous faerie, was distracted once again with her idiotic thoughts.

As Lacuna got ready, Sonai suddenly muttered, "Maybe she's the Olan?"

Lacuna stopped in horror. Olan—she knows what the Olan is? Would she finally get the answers she was looking for?

Before Lacuna could say anything else, the door knob to room 235 C suddenly turned. Lacuna quickly retracted her sword and placed it back in its pocket-sized sheath.

Standing in the doorway was a somewhat pale girl, much shorter than Lacuna. She was wearing pajamas and bunny slippers despite the time only being late afternoon.

"I thought I heard people talking out here," she yawned. "I'm sorry, I just woke up from a nap." The girl sluggishly looked down the hallway, suddenly perking up when she saw Sonai. "Oh, hey Sonai!" she shouted while waving frantically. Sonai waved back calmly with an awkward smirk.

Did Sonai have friends?

"Oh my god, do you two know each other?" The girl was a lot more excited than she was mere seconds ago. What happened to her tiredness?

Lacuna was about to tell her no, but Sonai suddenly spoke up as she walked towards them. "Kinda. I was talking to her about the dorms." She threw her arm over Lacuna's shoulder and grinned at the girl. "Right before you woke up, we were talking and stuff."

Technically they were, but technically they weren't. Lacuna knew that fae couldn't lie, and that their unusual wording often allowed them to get away with telling half-truths, but the extent of Sonai's felt almost too falsified. Honestly, who would believe that? Nothing about their fight sounded like a casual conversation between acquaintances.

The girl analyzed Sonai's movement around Lacuna quizzically. "Aww, that's so nice of you! Speaking of dorms, I'm actually waiting for my roommate to arrive."

Of course… right as she was in the process of working.

"I'm the person you've been waiting for," Lacuna said with a sigh. She hoped the girl wouldn't realize it was from annoyance.

"Oh hi! Come on in!" The girl began frantically ushering Lacuna inside the room. "By the way, my name is Ala."

"Lacuna Rae Cryoni."

"Oh wow, full name, how formal!" Ala looked past Lacuna and shouted "bye" to Sonai.

Lacuna also looked back at Sonai. After waving bye to Ala, she mouthed "good luck" to Lacuna, nodding with a mischievous smile. By the window she stood in front of, a single dove was perched, preening its feathers with an air of nonchalant pristineness.

As Ala pulled her into the room, Lacuna began to realize that the Oracle was absolutely correct about the time she would need for this mission. This was going to take a while.

CHAPTER 3

L acuna found herself standing on water in a pitch black room. The dark liquid appeared to go on forever. Lacuna trudged forwards, searching for an exit. Her body felt sluggish, like it was being weighed down by the water beneath her feet. She walked for a few minutes. Many hours. Many days. Perhaps weeks. Maybe months. Yet no matter how far she walked, she couldn't find an exit. Maybe water went on forever.

That is, until she spotted a small light in the distance.

It didn't lead out of the black room with water. Instead, it led to another spot in its eternal source. As Lacuna looked down, she saw a figure underneath the surface. One with the same features as her, but much brighter. The only glowing shape in the room. They appeared tranquil, eyes closed and irrevocably still. Lacuna wasn't sure if they were alive, but as she leaned to one side to get a closer look, the figure leaned with her. As she leaned to the other side, they leaned with her again. After a while she began to wonder, "Is this my reflection?"

She had asked herself this question, the words never physically leaving her mouth. Then she got closer to the water, face mere inches away from the eyelids of the being underneath its surface.

"No." Golden eyes shot open, waterlogged and reflective of everything she couldn't understand. "We are not reflections of one another. But we are kin." Then the being grabbed her arm, dragging her underneath the water's surface.

What Lacuna saw down there should've been entirely incomprehensible to her. It almost was. Yet she could vaguely remember the smell of the ocean, the taste of chocolate, and the sound of laughter. She could recall the first two senses from her days in Revenali.

But on the island, people rarely laughed around her. So who was laughing at her now?

Lacuna awoke in her dorm room to the sound of Ala snoring, pushing the bizarre dream into the back of her mind. Sitting up, she scanned the room, looking for any signs of a faerie nearby.

There was a dove on the windowsill.

She rushed over and scared it off, then closed the window softly. After a few minutes of waiting for it to come back, wondering if it was truly the cause of her nightmare, she laid back down. Despite her tiredness, Lacuna wasn't sure if she could go back to sleep.

That morning was filled with thoughts of another fae: Sonai Adalim. Since their first encounter, it had been a few weeks since the two of them had seen each other. Outside of strange dreams, Lacuna's life in college was going rather well. So far, she'd been passing her classes. She'd also gotten along better with Ala than she thought she would.

The best way to describe Ala in one word would be *cheery*. She was always smiling, possessing a non-stop energy. Ala always had something to say that most people—who of course, were not Lacuna—would consider funny. It was as if she made friends everywhere she went. While walking with Ala to her afternoon geometry class on Tuesday, which happened to be in the same direction and time as Lacuna's algebra class, there was rarely a moment where she didn't wave *"hi"* to someone walking by. And a lot of people walked by. How she knew so many people? Lacuna would never understand.

On the topic of things that Lacuna didn't know, Sonai's current location was one of them. She couldn't seem to find her anywhere. A few days ago, she tried to check the other dormitories, then realized she needed a specific keycard. For safety reasons, students couldn't enter buildings that they weren't housed in. If she wanted to see Sonai, she would have to make an entry request. Either way, she had no idea which building she lived in, thus her plan to catch the Feomin off guard was scrapped.

After that, she simply searched around campus, looking in the library, the auditorium, a few well-known lecture halls, and a couple of the dining halls. She proceeded to do this every day. Yet, no matter where or how often she searched, Lacuna just couldn't find her. This was especially odd since Sonai had walked right up to her during their previous battle.

Why was she being elusive now?

Lacuna also began to notice all of the weird looks she was getting from other students. Her frequent checks for Sonai made it obvious to people that she was looking for someone, even if they had no idea who it was. Today in her sleep deprived state, a man came up to her while she was searching a wall in the dining hall for clues. He asked her if she was "ok."

Of course she was! She felt that it was an odd question to ask. Albeit, Lacuna might have been looking at the wall for quite a while, but it wasn't any of his business anyway. And she obviously couldn't tell any non-Arius that she was looking for a faerie.

"I'm simply observing the magnificent texture of these walls," she lied.

The man gave her an even more perplexed look before slowly walking away. She would need to be more careful, or else her cover could be blown.

Eventually, Ala entered the dining hall too. But unlike the man, she questioned Lacuna's motives more deeply. In her presence, Lacuna professed that her glances at walls were simply due to her being deep in thought. However, she did tell Ala that her more thorough searches of the school were specifically because she was looking for Sonai. Of course, she didn't tell her the exact reason why she attempted to seek her out, just that she was looking.

"I'm sorry I can't help you find her. I don't have any classes with her, and I don't know her number."

Surprised, Lacuna asked, "I thought you and Sonai were friends?"

"Nope, we're more so just peers. Or maybe even less than that." She sighed sadly. "The only reason I know her is because we met during freshman orientation last year."

"I see…"

"Yeah. I mean she seems like a really helpful person, but she can be kind of… rude sometimes."

"What do you mean?"

Ala got closer to Lacuna, whispering. "Every once in a while, I wondered if she'd been taught any, like, manners as a kid. She doesn't say please, or thank you, or sorry to anyone! Like, there was this time last year when we were walking together, and she flipped a guy off because he asked her to apologize for something she was one-hundred percent in the wrong for!" She gave Lacuna an awkward smile, simultaneously amused by her tale, yet abashed that she felt this way about the event. "I'm not going to get into the specifics of that situation, just that it was really weird. And again, she's super helpful, and usually pretty chill. But if I'm totally honest, she's kinda strange to me. It's also why I've never asked for her number, otherwise I would've tried to hang out with her more already."

"I see. If I had her phone number, then this process would be much easier," Lacuna mumbled, feeling defeated. "I was interested in getting to know her more."

Ala looked at her with a quizzical look and a small smile. "Oop? Are you saying you're interested in her?"

Lacuna knew there was supposed to be an odd connotation behind her words, but she couldn't determine what being *interested in* Sonai could mean. Phrases like this weren't used around the Oracle. And she was always around the Oracle.

Rather than ask for the meaning, she settled for contesting Ala's statement indirectly. "I am interested in figuring out where she went, because I can't find her anywhere on campus. That's all."

"Ok, ok!" Ala held her hands up defensively as she giggled. Lacuna really needed to figure out what that phrase meant before she saw Ala again. Evident by her reaction, she doubted that whatever it implied would make her happy. For now, the two of them walked towards their only shared class of the week.

Despite her Arius-related troubles, Lacuna was walking with Ala again the next day, except this time it wasn't to any classes. Ala really wanted to show her some of the new flowers that Podim University's gardening club had planted in the courtyard recently. This was a large spacious area located directly in the middle of Podim's main academic buildings, which appeared as two rectangular U shapes that faced one another like magnets. Lacuna was often told that the courtyard was frequently filled with students. As expected, it was today too.

So many students, studying, chatting, and watching the flowers Ala just told her about. Ala was completely right about how pretty the flowers were. Various colors, like an oil painting, surrounded the garden of students. Lacuna was nearly mesmerized.

Nearly, because a very familiar figure moved directly in front of her line of sight for the flowers.

"Sonai!" Lacuna seethed. Finally, there she was after avoiding her for so long. She dashed towards her, prepared to drag her away from the crowd.

Sonai was just trying to enjoy the flowers. However, she failed to notice the mad Arius dashing at her like an Olympic track star.

"What is she doing? That idiot was gonna blow her cover coming at her like this!"

acuna lunged to grab her. Surprised, Sonai locked arm around Lacuna's shoulder, then her neck in order to trap her subtly. Hopefully, it just looked like a hug.

"Ahh, it's you again!" Sonai said somewhat loudly with a crooked smile. She hugged Lacuna tighter.

Lacuna struggled against her hold. "Release me!" she growled.

Sonai leaned close to her ear, not speaking directly into it. She whispered, "What on earth are you doing? You're an Arius aren't you? Why are you rushing at me in public?"

Matching her volume, Lacuna replied, "I wasn't going to fight you in here, but you have been avoiding me. I plan to take you to a different location."

Someone shouts from across the courtyard, running in their direction. It's Ala. She calls out, "So this is why you ran from me so suddenly." She stood in front of them, panting, and placed her hands on her knees. "Man Lacuna, you run *fast!*"

The two girls look at her stiffly.

"So Sonai, how have you been?" Ala asked once she collected herself.

"Pretty good." She releases her hold on Lacuna slightly, putting her arm around the other girl's shoulder instead. It looked more casual than the borderline chokehold she had on her a few seconds ago.

"Is that all?" Lacuna asked angrily. "Where were you? I couldn't find you anywhere around Podim University."

"Aww. Did ya' miss me?" She looked up at her with a grin.

Ala looked between the two of them with a questioning look, which quickly morphed into a small smile. "Um... so how's the courtyard, guys?"

"Fine," the two said in unison, continuing to look at one another. Sonai, grinning as per usual and Lacuna, still annoyed by her personality. They stood this way for a few seconds. Then, Lacuna suddenly grabbed the collar of Sonai's shirt, dragging her away.

Ala observed the scene deep in thought. At first it was simply a few short lived thoughts, but now? She was really beginning to wonder what was going on between those two...

Back inside one of the main campus buildings, Lacuna looked around the area. There was not a person insight within the long hallway. She dragged Sonai into the nearest women's restroom and proceeded to knock on each of the stalls. The close was clear here. Lacuna let go of Sonai's collar, walking over to the main door of the restroom to lock it. Once finished, she pulled out a retractable short-sword. In an instant, she rushed at Sonai, pinning her to the white tile walls with an audible *thud*.

"There's no way you're suppose' to be the Arius to assassinate me." The sword pressed closer to her neck. She stared directly into the eyes of her assassin. "Constantly attacking me in public like this? Do you want to be discovered?"

Lacuna was silent. Focused, hopefully near emotionless. Just like she needed to be. As the Oracle expected.

The flames behind Sonai's eyes, which she originally thought were just a trick of the light, appear to burn brighter. If they were really her imagination, she couldn't stand looking at them any longer. It was time to finish this. But before Lacuna killed her, she needed to have an answer to the one question she's been wanting to ask someone for a while...

"What is the Olan?" she demanded.

"Who sent you?" Sonai tilted her head forward, pressing a bit deeper against the knife. Exposing Lacuna to more of the fire.

"Answer my question."

"Mmm? Nah." Her expression stayed the same.

"Answer my question." The sternness of her voice increased.

"Why would I? I don't answer questions for murderers." She smiled at her, teeth—no—fangs glinting under the fluorescent lights of the bathroom. "So, who sent you? And I don't mean the main agency for other assassins like you. You aren't a normal Arius."

Although it's said that fae can't lie, the sound of Sonai's statement made the original concept seem improbable. Lacuna was a normal Arius. She knew it. It had to be true. She received a proper Arius education from the Oracle. She learned how to fight, recognize, and track down fae just like everyone else. There were plenty of other Arius in Revenali who could use magic. She wasn't unique or different in any way.

But, one could argue there were—faults—in her current mission. And anything the Oracle did definitely wasn't normal. She knew this well.

And she didn't want Sonai to know that.

So, she refused to answer. Still unwavering, Lacuna asked, "Have you ever had a knife to your throat before?"

"Have you ever been in the presence of a faerie before?"

"Stop deflecting."

"How about you stop instead?"

"No, I don't think I will... Olan."

Lacuna tensed at the sound of the word. Did the Olan really have something to do with her?

In her slight moment of distraction, Sonai took the opportunity to attack Lacuna. Moving to the right, she escaped the blade of the knife, letting it slide across her neck where a cut should've been made. Should've, but it was if her skin appeared thicker now.

No, not if. It was definitely much thicker now. She was currently in her *true* form.

Her form as a fae was similar to her human form. Same hair, same skin tone, same face and body structure. But she was obviously very different. Just as it was illustrated in the Oracle's book, her long dark hair contrasted with sharp white fangs. Sharp yet twisting horns protruded from her hair. Her elvish ears and languid black tail flicked a little with repulsive creepiness. Nearly vanta-black hands faded into a dark gradient, further emphasized by sharp, similarly black talons. Her darkened scleras laid behind blood-red irises. So bright in real life. The usual fire in her eyes was at its peak.

She grabbed Lacuna by the neck, throwing her to the floor. Upon hitting the tile, her skull felt like it was buzzing, ears ringing. It took her a few seconds to regain focus, but once she did, the sight she saw was burned into her memories.

Peering down at her were the demonic eyes of a Feomin. Sonai. This was what Sonai truly looked like. This malevolent, twisted humanoid form, a presence more striking than the dim fluorescents of the bathroom. Smiling down at her, hair cascading, ensnaring Lacuna and forcing her directly into her fiery eyes. Yet it also conveniently shielded her from the fluorescent lights that would amplify her head ache. In fact she might have a concussion, because the thoughts in her mind didn't feel quite right for this situation. This was what Sonai strength was really like. What could Lacuna do against her? She could kill her right here and now. Was she going to fail?

So many emotions were flying through Lacuna's aching head. Anger, disappointment, something tingly in nature that she couldn't quite recognize. But worst of all, she felt fear. Not nervousness or hints of surprise. Genuine fear. An emotion she hadn't felt in a very long time.

But she didn't show it. Or at least, she thought she didn't.

"You know, at first I thought you were gonna be like all of the other Arius I've fought before. Trying to act like you weren't human so you could 'kill' better. But now I realize you're the most human-like out of all of 'em." She giggled. "And you know what's funny? You're probably the least human out of all of them too!"

Lacuna snarled at her, angry at her assumption, yet powerless to do anything about it. Sonai stopped leaning over her, reverting back into her human form. She sighed, still looking down at Lacuna from what was now a foot away. Her expression was more serious and docile; in a way, somewhat sad. It was an expression that Lacuna had not thought Sonai was capable of having on her normally leering face.

"What did they do to you?" The question was muttered, as if she didn't really mean to say it out loud. After a few seconds, she stood up fully and remarked, "I'm not gonna kill you. I'm not sure if I'm supposed to anymore." She crossed her arms.

Lacuna looked up at her confused; the cold tile pressed against her head made Sonai's words seem even more shocking to hear.

"And if you're trying to find any information about whatever the Olan is, I'm not the one you should ask. In fact, no one knows what the Olan is other than the Queen." She then strode towards the door, unlocking it swiftly. Leaving Lacuna alone in the dim bathroom, with an aching head, convoluted emotions, and an enemy still undefeated.

CHAPTER 4

A week had passed since the bathroom incident with Sonai. Luckily, Lacuna did not have a concussion, yet she would have no progress to show the Oracle during the upcoming Somnium Conference. Later today, all available   Arius were to return to Revenali for an in-depth meeting regarding the overall   state of Earth. This type of event only happened once a year in Revenali. Lacuna considered it to be one of the only interesting occasions within the country, since most Arius didn't celebrate holidays.

Earlier today, she met up with Jordan again for her first monthly check in. While he was away, she did some research. His skills were among the best, and knowledge on fae was nearly akin to that of the Oracle. Responsible for the extermination of over fifty fae: no wonder he was a member of the Runic Arius. He would have to be someone that Lacuna looked up to more often.

They met up at a cafe near campus. It was also across the street from Cane Corso Coffee. Horrible placement in Lacuna's opinion.

Just like the abandoned coffee shop, her progress was also horrible. Once confronted about it, she tried to reason with Jordan, explaining that Sonai was simply too elusive for her to catch off guard. Hoping that he would take her word for it. She couldn't quite say that Sonai was too strong, since she had yet to truly fight her in a full-on battle away from civilian eyes. Yet her explanation simply got her a questioning look from Jordan. While the two of them sat, waiting for their respective coffee orders to arrive at the small spruce table, Jordan asked her a strange question.

"Do you truly understand the hierarchy of fae, Lacuna?"

"Of course, sir." She stood up straighter, although her posture was already near perfect.

"Do you understand how the powers of Feomin work in comparison to other faeries?"

"To be truthful, not entirely sir." She glanced around the building, keeping her voice low. "I understand that their level of magic energy is much higher than all other fae. I know that this allows them to transcend the Veil for extreme lengths of time. I also understand that this level of magical energy makes them much stronger than any other fae, other than the Faerie Queen, of course." She didn't entirely believe the words she stated could be used to describe Sonai. Was she really that powerful? "Other than this, my knowledge is very limited."

"I see…" he remarked. Their coffees then arrived at the table; Jordan thanked the waitress before taking a sip. The sip was short, the bitter coffee striking his tongue disappointingly. He grabbed five packets of sugar from the table's center, ripping them open in a calm yet evidently dissatisfied manner. Without looking up from his coffee, Jordan said, "As you should know, there are two courts within the ealm of the fae: Seelie and Unseelie. Good and bad. Or so, that is the way most would like to categorize them as." He took another sip from his coffee. More satisfied now. "However, this categorization isn't always accurate. When the concepts were first created by witches, it was based on how likely a certain type of faerie was to trick or hurt you. 'Though, Revenalian's soon came to realize that these categories didn't really matter when it came to our jobs as assassins. Yet even in the present day, the categories are still used."

Lacuna took a sip of her own coffee. It was bitter, but that was exactly how she liked it. Uncomplicated, no need to add anything more. But in terms of information, that was the opposite of what she needed right now. She knew all of this information already, and Jordan knew that too. So, where was he going with this conversation?

"Feomin are often categorized as Unseelie fae due to their demonic appearance. Yet when looking at their mannerisms, they're one of the least likely to play tricks on humans. Many try to blend in as much as possible with civilians."

"Why?"

"Our current researchers aren't quite sure. However, so far we do know that Feomin are considered to be the something of a right hand of the Faerie Queen. They can enter the Veil willingly and without much effort. Perfect choice for when work needs to be done from beyond the other side."

"I see. I have to say, the information that was provided to me before my mission was quite vague. Does Revenali have any more information on Sonai Adalim, the Feomin I'm currently hunting?"

"Not exactly. However, outside of the fae realm, the magical prowess of Feomin should somewhat lessen. For most of our captive fae, this happened, however, we're still not sure if her magic is actually as extreme as the claims from witches make it out to be. That being said, it's likely that it still outmatches humans."

Lacuna nodded. Again, it felt as though she had heard all of this information already. She wanted fresher information, something that could give her an edge over Sonai. Something that could make her easier to track down. Or at least something that would make her less prone to Sonai's distractions.

Lacuna felt somewhat disappointed with herself. Despite all of the Oracle's teachings, she was still just as distracted as a child. What was wrong with her? Her focus, constantly slipping. Becoming angered by simple taunts. Wanting to know more about a concept she's not even sure she's supposed to have questions about. At this rate, there would be no chance at receiving a position among the Runic Arius, let alone, at freeing the human realm from Sonai's blight. She stared at her coffee in silence, right as Jordan also sipped at his.

Out of the corner of her eye, she saw him grab another sugar packet.

Around an hour later, the two of them left the cafe, walking down towards Cane Corso Coffee. Upon entering the nearby alleyway, Jordan took out his portal gem and opened the portal. Going through the vortex was as dizzying as it was the first time, a kaleidoscope of colors swirling within the portal, whisking the two Arius back to Revenali.

No matter the time period, Revenali always remained the same. Thus, her life within the Oracle's temple was often uneventful. After hours of studying and strength training, she would often sit in her room and stare at the bare ceiling. Yet, there was one time that Lacuna found herself playing outside with another child. She was around eleven at the time, the other kid many years younger than her—perhaps around six. They were passing a ball around the temple entrance, standing on the wide landing of the staircase that led up to the doorway. Technically, Lacuna was only babysitting the young boy while his mother, a maid within the temple, went shopping for the Oracle. The ball flew through pink ombre sky, finding itself caught in Lacuna's hands after a few passes between the two children.

The boy suddenly spoke up, excitedly telling Lacuna about his dog. She couldn't remember its name. He rambled on about how cute the dog was; his delight when it was given to the family. And then he proceeded to talk about his family. The boy and Lacuna sat against the large brick railing that surrounded the temple's stairway; just as large and winding as the stairs themselves. He told her about his sister and brother. Then his dad. And finally, his mom. It was only this part of the conversation that Lacuna actually remembered.

"You know…" He played with a few pebbles on the ground. "Mommy's gonna come to pick me up soon. Is your mom gonna come to get you too?"

"I live here at the temple. I don't have a mother or father."

"Wait, really?" He stared at her in surprise. "Do you like living here? Because I don't think I would. The temple seems so cold and empty."

"I don't mind the temple's atmosphere."

"What does atmosphere mean?"

Calmly, she replied, "It refers to the air and space of an area. I'm saying that the way in which the temple feels and looks does not bother me."

"Ok." He turned to look at her. "You know a lot of big words."

"Atmosphere is not a big word."

"Yes it is. I bet it has a lot of letters."

"The word atmosphere only has ten letters. You need to read more books."

"No! I don't like reading! You sound like my mom." He paused. "Um… are you sure you don't have a mom or dad? 'Cause my mom usually teaches me big words."

"Again, I don't have any parents."

"My big brother told me that everyone has a mommy and a daddy."

"The Oracle informed me when I was five years old that I do not have a mother or father, unlike you seem to claim I do."

"Is my big brother wrong?"

"I'm unsure of the answer to that question."

"Oh."

The two of them sat in silence for a moment, the child deep in thought. He suddenly perked up and asked, "Maybe the temple person with the mask who let me play with you today is your mom?" His expression shifted in a puzzled way. "Or… dad?"

"Are you referring to the Oracle?"

"Yes it is. I bet it has a lot of letters."

"The word atmosphere only has ten letters. You need to read more books."

"No! I don't like reading! You sound like my mom." He paused. "Um… are you sure you don't have a mom or dad? 'Cause my mom usually teaches me big words."

"Again, I don't have any parents."

"My big brother told me that everyone has a mommy and a daddy."

"The Oracle informed me when I was five years old that I do not have a mother or father, unlike you seem to claim I do."

"Is my big brother wrong?"

"I'm unsure of the answer to that question."

"Oh."

The two of them sat in silence for a moment, the child deep in thought. He suddenly perked up and asked, "Maybe the temple person with the mask who let me play with you today is your mom?" His expression shifted in a puzzled way. "Or… dad?"

"Are you referring to the Oracle?"

"I think so? That person wears a blue mask right?"

"Yes. And perhaps you should refer to the Oracle more formally. They are not a random person after all."

"Okie." He didn't seem to take her suggestion with much seriousness. He got up from his spot. "Do you wanna see me do a backflip?"

"Are you sure you can do a backflip?"

"I've been practicing at home, so I should be able to." He ran over to the middle of the gradious staircase landing. "Ok, here I go in 3…2…"

"Reno!"

The child, Reno, stopped his backflip attempt to run in the direction of the voice. Lacuna turned her attention as well. A woman she had never seen before was walking up the temple's gradious staircase. She stopped at one of the smaller landings, visible from where Lacuna was sitting, gently dropping the grocery bags she had on hand.

"Mommy!" Reno jumped into the arms of the woman. Lacuna couldn't help but notice how similar they both looked. Hazel eyes. Tanned skin. The same thick, curly hair.

The woman looked at her, gesturing for her to come over to her. Even from a few feet away, she knew that the woman was much taller than her. But upon standing directly next to her, she was extremely tall, nearly the Oracle's height. Lacuna, the small child she was, looked up at the woman blankly, tilting her head.

She handed Lacuna two grocery bags. "Here are the items that their Highness wanted." She spoke in a sweet, calming voice. Crouching down to match Lacuna's eyes, she said, "Thank you for watching Reno. I know he can be a handful, but I hope he wasn't too much trouble."

Reno, stunned by his mother's implicit accusation, exclaimed, "I wasn't any trouble! I was good today, Mommy."

The lady chuckled, voice tranquil. "I know, baby. Don't worry." She patted his head, ruffling his curls. In response Reno put his hands on his head, feebly trying to stop her as he pretended to whine, giggling.

Lacuna didn't understand what she felt looking at the sight. She found herself staring at the two, a heavy feeling swirling with her chest. She glared intensely at Reno, vaguely wanting to be the one whose head full of curls and coils was ruffled by a tall kind lady who looked like her.

Reno and his mother waved goodbye to Lacuna, finally descending the mountain towards the setting sun. Lacuna stood there for a moment, holding the grocery bags, watching them walk away. They were still laughing at jokes Lacuna had no knowledge about, created over the years as mother and son.

The Oracle was silently reading a book in their office, not acknowledging Lacuna's presence when she entered. She dropped off the items, preparing to walk back to her room and do nothing for the rest of the evening. But then Reno's mother appeared in her mind. Her kind words, her caring attentiveness, and her calming voice.

The Oracle praised Lacuna when she was observant during her lessons. They always paid attention to her. The Oracle's voice was pretty calm; smooth like silk. And according to Reno, the most important factor of a parental figure was whether or not they taught you big words. The Oracle evidently did this, so maybe they really were...

Lacuna walked over to their desk. The Oracle continued to read, supposedly engrossed in their book. But she knew they were paying attention. They always were.

"Are you my mommy?" The question was stated without emotion.

They finally looked up, silent.

"Or, are you my daddy?"

Clearing their throat, the Oracle asked, "Lacuna. First, I must ask where and when on earth you decided to add words such as mommy and daddy to your vocabulary?" While focusing on Lacuna, they closed the book, not bookmarking the page. "Second, you should already know the answer to those questions. I am definitely not one of your parents. The temple assistants are your main caretakers. I hardly qualify as a guardian for you in any regard." Their voice became quieter, their gaze more direct. Lacuna could sense a flash of emotion past the porcelain mask.

"I could never be your mother or father. Nor could I act as a replacement for them, whoever they might be."

CHAPTER 5

Lacuna found herself skittering around the ballroom, unsure of what to do. The Somnium Conference had begun, the Runic Palace swelling with Arius, hungry for both knowledge and the Rune family's expensive cuisine. People bustled about the grand glittering room, its marble floors and gilded chandeliers shining with ancient anticipation. A wide empty stage, short in terms of height, was against the northward wall. This wall was decorated with large elaborately designed windows. The architecture within the palace was unlike the rest of Revenali. From the outside, it matched the rest of the country's simple Mediterranean sandstone bases, with the palace's additional pearlescent accents displaying its status in a way similar to Oracle's Temple. However, its towers were tall and curved, like tree branches. And the inside was that of notable European royalty. Even the Oracle's Temple, in all of its grandeur, didn't stick out this much from atop Altare Mountain.

What answers were other Arius within the room looking for? What progress in eliminating the threat of fae had they made? Was anyone else assigned to fight a faerie as strong as hers? Lacuna glanced at the mystic swords and ornate shields the warriors had strapped across their backs–that of which were clothed by elegant dresses and suits. All symbols of their status and skill. Things that Lacuna did not have. Lacuna looked down at her simple temple robes, the only fancy item that was in her relatively bare closet.

She felt out of place in all aspects.

Lacuna continued to skitter about, eventually making her way towards the concession table. The area smelled of peppers and various seasonings, like an Italian restaurant. Grabbing a plate, she globbed on a pile of mashed potatoes and grabbed a couple chicken tenders, ignoring the fancy vegetable stir-fry. She proceeded to eat her mound near the table, still standing. Using one of the orate forks, she quickly shoveled potatoes into her mouth, holding her plate close to her chin. Some of the nobles stared at her direction before quickly going back to their business. Even surrounded by fellow Arius she was still stared at just like she was at Podim's campus.

Lacuna rolled her eyes.

She wondered where the Oracle was right now. They came to the palace with her before walking off on their own a couple minutes later. As one of Revenali's most important figures, they were to give a speech tonight alongside the Rune family.

"Are the mashed potatoes really that good?" asked a robust voice directly to her left.

"Hm-mm!" Lacuna quickly turned, startled, cheeks stuffed with potato.

The woman laughed, the sound echoing throughout the ballroom. Many of the nobles turned and looked in Lacuna's direction again, for a little longer this time.

She appeared to be around the same height as Lacuna, maybe a few centimeters taller. Yet this increase in height was most likely due to the knee-high combat boots she was wearing. At a fancy dinner party, she was dressed for battle. Even among the many sword welding Arius in the room, her curved double blades, symbols of the Rune family, stood out the most. The woman in question was Morana Rune, leader of Revenali. Notorious for her battles against fearsome faeries, her dedication to Arius education and one of the youngest leaders in the history of Revenali. Truly a follower of Marcus Revenali's teachings.

"So, how's the party?" she asked with a smile.

Lacuna roughly swallowed her mashed potatoes and bowed. "It has been well, High Arius Rune."

"You don't have to be so formal! You can just call me Morana."

Lacuna awkwardly nodded at the recommendation, unsure of what to make of Morana Rune's sudden appearance in front of her.

Upon seeing her silence, Morana's smile faded. "You know, despite the…fanciness… of this party, it really is just a boring meeting for old people to discuss nothing and talk *at* each other. You were the only interesting one in the room, which is why I approached you."

Lacuna mostly disagreed with her first statement. While the long drawn out speeches were definitely boring, the atmosphere was invigorating. Plus, the notoriety of the party provided Lacuna with a much needed disruption in her often very boring life. And the food was great.

The second statement left her even more disappointed. She knew there was no way that the leader of Revenali would genuinely want to talk with someone unknown like her, especially not at the Somnarium Conference of all places. Yet being used as a device for her entertainment was somewhat demeaning. The action reminded her of someone that a leader of Revenali should, preferably, never be a reminder of. Lacuna guessed this was a minor example of what people meant when they said *'never meet your heroes.'*

Suddenly, a voice echoed around the ballroom through a microphone, positioned on the stage. Lacuna saw that it was the Oracle, ready to give a speech. The early afternoon light reflected off of the shiny marble floor, an additional glow directed onto the Oracle. They cleared their throat, signifying the arrival of the news everyone was here for.

"Good afternoon, great Arius of the Republic of Revenali. I hope that everyone has been enjoying the festivities. I know that I have!" The statement was said calmly, without a hint of any actual joy. Multiple people in the room chuckled. Lacuna found nothing funny about it. She knew the Oracle barely participated. They made this same statement every year.

"Now, we must get into the actual matters of the notorious Somnium Conference. First, we shall start with the statistical updates. As of last year, over two-hundred witches have been eliminated world-wide, along with their faerie familiars." The crowd cheered and clapped. "I must ask that everyone hold their applause until the end. To continue, around five-hundred independent faeries were eliminated world-wide, with nearly three-hundred of them coming from the United States of America alone. I would like to give extra congratulations to all Arius currently stationed in America for their efforts. You may all congratulate your peers as well during this time." The crowd once again erupted into claps and cheers, friends patting each other on the back.

"Are you stationed in America?" Morana asked despite the cacophony.

Lacuna nodded.

"Nice! Keep up the good work!" Morana patted her lightly on the shoulder.

The acknowledgement felt good.

The Oracle held up their hand to signal an end to the crowd's excitement. Upon quiet settling again, they continued. "Now, I shall bring the qualitative data updates onto the floor. Firstly, large numbers of Red-Caps have been spotted in Sweden. Although large numbers of blood-thirsty fae are often spotted around this time of year, the number seems to be increasing to new, previously unforeseen heights. Red-Caps are especially a danger. However, the Revenalian Council is currently unable to pin-point why such a large number of them have appeared in Sweden. I ask that any Arius stationed within the country provide a report to the council on any additional information. As of right now, we ask that any Arius stationed in areas with Red-Cap sightings stay extra vigilant."

The Oracle suddenly looked directly at Lacuna. "And on the topic of dangerous fae…"

Oh no.

"… I must announce that there was recently a Feomin sighting in America." The crowd clamored in surprise. "However, we have a strong, capable Arius taking care of the issue. I would like to congratulate my apprentice, Lacuna Cryoni for her current efforts!" Most of the crowd clapped aimlessly, having no idea who she was or where she was in the room. Some of them did turn to look at her, based on where the Oracle's marked face was titled.

Morana patted her on the back a little harder this time. "Oh my God! Congratulations! How's the mission going?" The few people who were actually looking in her direction nodded, also wanting to know the answer.

"Progress is being made." The simple answer was all she could muster through her embarrassment.

Morana was unimpressed, but didn't push any further.

"The final thing that I would like to announce before handing the stage over to the Rune family is that the history being created here, in this very room, on this very island, is special. Every single one of you is walking the same path as the esteemed Marcus Revenali, working hard to eliminate the covert dangers of our beautiful world. Taking pain away from everyday citizens who have no idea of the beasts that secretly plague them. You would all make him very proud."

Lacuna hoped so.

"Thank you all for your time. And now I would like to introduce High Arius Morana Rune to the stage!" The crowd cheered again for the umpteenth time. Morana walked away from Lacuna without another word, the crowd parting like a wave as she marched through. Upon standing on stage, the crowd erupted, with cheers the loudest they had been all evening. For a second Lacuna thought the palace might shake.

"Good afternoon everyone," her voice echoed through the room like a general, much different than the playful tone was using with Lacuna. Actually, not like a general; she *was* a general.

"Thank you all for coming to the Somnium Conference in support of Revenali and the Rune Family. I'd like to announce that researchers within the family's ranks are currently creating new technologies involved with faeries crossing the Veil. Through our efforts we are beginning to discover ways to make fae stay on our side of the Veil by force." The crowd murmured, questioning her words. "This shall allow Arius to attack fae without them shifting back into their realm, allowing us to eliminate them without realm-related complications. The researchers have also discovered that using the technology could possibly send signals through the Veil when fae are tangled in it, which should hopefully influence other fae that are traveling to stay put."

Suddenly a small group of people, a few holding cameras and microphones of their own, rushed towards the front of the stage, pushing past the crowd insistently. One man within the group spoke into his mic, asking, "High Arius Morana Rune, there have been many rumors circulating around Revenali regarding the nature of this new technology. Even within the speech you gave just now, its description is extremely vague. Technologies with the power to forcefully hold fae within or beyond the Veil are unheard of!" His mic echoed from the force of anger. "Journalists and sociologists have argued that the technology may in fact be related to the topic of combining the realms in secret!" Animatedly, the crowd gasped at the accusation.

"Do you have anything to say about this?" Despite the fact that Morana had a microphone of her own, the man raised his towards her, perhaps symbolic.

"I can assure the people of Revenali that no such thing is going to happen with this machine. It simply holds fae that are captured by hand in a type of magic forcefield. There is absolutely no way it would ever be powerful enough to do something as extreme as merging the realms." Morana's voice became even more stern than it already was. "In fact I find it rather disrespectful that one would accuse the Rune family of committing such an act! We are proud followers of Marcus Revenali's message." Her unoccupied hand clenched into a fist as she proudly stated, "We would never betray him in such a way!" Much of the crowd calmed down, while others talked to their peers with confusion.

"To those who are still unsure, there is no need to worry. Although the technology is still new, substantial progress is being made in a short period of time. Within the next few months, there will be a showcase of the machine's powers directly for the public. And with that, I would like to conclude my announcement on behalf of the family." The crowd clapped as Morana stepped down from the stage. She stood next to the Oracle instead of reentering the crowd, making Lacuna slightly disappointed. But it was not only by Morana's actions, but by the Oracle's as well. The way in which they casually placed a gloved hand on her shoulder and laughed alongside her. Something they rarely did with Lacuna.

The rest of the Somnium Conference went by in a typical boring meeting fashion. Morana's grandfather came on stage and gave a speech about *perseverance* and the importance of Arius education. Then a random poet, who was supposedly very famous on the eastern side of Revenali, recited Marcus's speech *Beyond the Veil* in a very animated manner. It was most likely intended to be sophisticated and awe-inspiring, but it made quite a few people in the crowd laugh instead. Although Lacuna was not one of those people, Morana was. From where she was standing, it almost appeared as though the Oracle giggled as well. For the second time that evening.

Speaking of the Oracle, as the conference slowly wrapped up, they suddenly disappeared from the crowd while Lacuna scurried to get more potatoes. They left the ballroom to travel deeper into the palace.

The Oracle walked slowly through the halls, searching for the empty room they told Jordan to meet them in. Jordan was still somewhere in the crowded ballroom. Upon entering a nice looking office, they waited. There was a large window on the back wall of the office, letting the afternoon sunlight trail through. The ocean was also visible from here. The sight was reminiscent of the Oracle's own office at the temple.

After a few minutes, the man finally entered, somewhat weary.

"How have you been, Jordan Mitchels?"

"I've been fine. How about you, Your Highness?"

"Quite well. I'd like to apologize for having our meeting here at the castle. I originally intended to discuss the current matters at the temple, but the Somnium Conference got in the way of that." They sighed. "And as you know, I won't be able to clear much time in my schedule in the near future due to the rising situations involving violent fae."

"I completely understand, Your Highness. As requested, I would like to discuss Lacuna's current progress."

"Lovely," they chimed, walking over to the desk behind them. They sat down directly on the desk surface, smoothing their robes before doing so. "What is there to discuss?"

Jordan shifted on his heels slightly. Clearing his throat, he asked, "I don't mean to question your judgment, Your Highness, but are you sure Lacuna is the right Arius for this mission?"

"Very," the Oracle replied blankly.

"Of course you would believe that, Your Highness. It was you who made the decisions personally." He clears his throat. "That being said, her very first mission outside of training involves taking down a Feomin. She isn't making much progress, and of course she wouldn't with her current skill level. What I'm trying to say is that–"

The Oracle held up a hand, signaling Jordan to stop whatever unnecessary ramble he was about to go on about Lacuna. "Do you understand that Lacuna is very special compared to most of the other Arius here, Sir Mitchels?"

He gulps, fearing a lecture. "I had somewhat of a feeling."

The Oracle glares up at him through their mask. "*Very* special, Mitchels. It's why I had to raise her myself. If there is any Arius out there who is fit to go on a mission like this, Lacuna is absolutely the one." There's a shift in the atmosphere. "With the skills that she possesses, no extra units will be needed."

Jordan let the words settle in his mind. "Are you saying that she's…"

"I'm not saying anything." The weight of their eyes cut into him further. "However, if you believe I *did* say something, then it would be best to keep the thought to yourself."

Jordan found this odd. *Very odd*. But there was nothing he could do about his findings. It would be wiser of him to listen to the Oracle's… *suggestion*. This conversation was obviously not meant for the ears of other Arius. "I understand, Your Highness." He bowed low, hoping that his action might quell their anger.

"Good." Their glare seems to subside. "Now then, Lacuna wasn't the only topic I wanted to discuss with you…"

The two talked for a few more minutes about an incoming mission for Jordan. For what would hopefully only be the next month, he was going to investigate the sudden increase of *Red Caps* in Sweden.

An uncomfortable wave of energy flows over Jordan as he exits the room, preparing himself for his incoming mission, and the next time he has to meet with Lacuna.

CHAPTER 6

A s the cafeteria bustled with students, Lacuna turned her attention away from fast-food and onto the walls of the area. She traced a paper cloth along the ruddy brick, picking up a decade worth of dust in the process.

"She couldn't have come through here either…" Lacuna thought to herself, analyzing the dust.

In order for fae to reenter the faerie realm, special areas were needed. These spaces are often referred to as *liminal spaces*: areas in between known spaces, simply used as transitions from one place to another. At first, Lacuna thought that this part in the cafeteria would serve as a perfect liminal space for a wild faerie. It was far from the main area of the cafeteria, dimly lit, and stuck in an odd corner that created a small L-shaped hallway. At the end of the hallway was a metal door to the outer cafeteria area that looked as though it hadn't been used in years. Overall, the cafeteria looked more like an underground subway station than a space for hungry young adults.

Back in Revenali she witnessed how captured faeries escaped the realm through walls, taking the dirt and dust along with them, cleaning traces of themselves from normal human eyes. But it's that cleanliness which gives away the faeries location. So as Lacuna traced the paper along the wall, she expected it to be clean.

Lacuna definitely looked odd sitting near the strange hallway-wall and collecting dust samples. She hoped that the other students in the cafeteria would simply think she was an archaeology major or something similar.

She continued to search around, gaining stares in the process as per usual. The entire cafeteria looked like a brick warehouse, well lit, contrary to the hallway. The only thing that made it recognizable as a college cafeteria was its various fast food restaurant stands, all lined up along the northern and eastern walls. To the west, a few small windows lined the wall, allowing the cafeteria to refrain from looking like the hallway.

Lacuna found herself analyzing the southern wall, entirely bare. It also stood out in the cafeteria to her, but could it serve as a liminal space? Maybe when the cafeteria was empty?

Lacuna suddenly felt a tap on her shoulder. She whipped around, prepared for it to be Sonai. However, rather than sybaritic black curls, she saw plainly dyed auburn hair. It was Ala, her roommate who was just as cheery as usual.

"Whatcha doing?" she chimed, leaning towards her cleaned section of the wall.

"Nothing of importance. Just a personal experiment." Lacuna didn't look at her when she replied. Ala knew well and good that she wasn't an archeology major.

"What is it that you require me for?" Carefully, she looked towards her.

Ala laughed. "Has anyone ever told you that you talk really funny? Like a robot?" She held her hands behind her back, moving her weight from one foot to another. "Or maybe more like a rich lady from the 1800s?"

"Perhaps," she replied apathetically.

"Anyways, I wanted to ask you if you'd like to get lunch with me and a couple of friends? Originally, I wasn't gonna ask 'cause I thought you were getting lunch here, but then I realized you weren't really doing anything for real!" She looked down at the dusty cloth Lacuna held. "Soooo... how about it?"

"It's rather impolite of you to assume that what I'm currently doing is not important in some way. However..." She knew it was probably a lost clause to try and find a faerie in a full cafeteria. "I shall accept your offer."

"Yay! So how do you feel about 1:30 today?"

"That should work. I have no classes from then until 3:00 P.M."

Ala rubbed her hands together with a fake mischievousness. "Perfect! Well, I'll see you at May's Cafe at 1:30." She waved goodbye as she dashed away quickly.

Their interaction was simple and vague, occurring in a manner Lacuna felt was way too quick. She had a feeling Ala nearly forgot to tell her the cafe name. However, she didn't, and that was all that mattered. Now she had one more class to attend before lunch. It was currently 12:15.

A few minutes later, Lacuna was sitting in a lecture hall, writing down algebra notes. The lesson was boring as per usual, but she had experienced even more boring lessons back in Revenali with the Oracle. The seats within the room wrapped around like a half-eaten donut. Donut... Lacuna felt her stomach growl. Did the cafe Ala wanted her to visit after this lesson sell donuts? Maybe she would allow herself to indulge in one simple pleasure...

Lacuna looked to the seats across the room, tired of looking at the quadratic formula. As she did, something caught her eye.

Hair, the color of tanzanite, was no longer hidden by a hood. The girl that Lacuna had run into during her first day on campus was looking diligently at her notebook with another girl sitting next to her. The other girl was just as colorful, with box braids in a swirly pink-to-black ombre laying over her shoulders in pig-tails. The blue haired girl gazed in Lacuna's direction, eyes becoming wide when she saw her. And those eyes, that Lacuna couldn't see at first, gave something *very* important away.

To the untrained eye, her eyes were normal. A very pretty shade of blue, but relatively normal. Nevertheless, any Arius would know the truth.

This girl wasn't human. Another fae was loitering in Podim University.

The girl next to her appeared normal enough; her eyes lacked the sort of sparkle that most fae's did. But Lacuna couldn't be entirely sure. Looking at her closely, Lacuna could see she was wearing a strange bracelet, possibly made of iron. However, if she were a faerie, it wouldn't be possible for her to wear it. There were more factors leading towards the girl not being a fae than there were to her being one. But no matter if she was or was not a fae, there were currently two present under her watch, Sonai and the blue haired girl.

She continued to stare subconsciously at her for the rest of class. It would be best to avoid losing track of another faerie under her watch.

Around an hour later, Lacuna found herself in front of May's Cafe, looking around for Ala. The cafe building was small; its interior appeared cozy from where Lacuna was standing outside. Outside was also where most of the picnic style seating was, accented by a large floral yard where customers could set up their own seating. A few yards away was a tall iron fence, separating the cafe area from a large forest. As Lacuna continued to glance around, she finally saw Ala sitting with two other girls on a nearby picnic blanket. As Lacuna approached them, she realized it was the two girls from her Algebra lecture hall. So they were friends of hers?

"Hey Lacuna, I'm so glad you could make it," Ala exclaimed. "Oh! I'm assuming you haven't met Tobi and Kelisha yet?" She gestured to the two girls.

They both turn around, the girl with the pink braids saying, "Hello, I'm Kelisha. It's nice to meet you," with a smile.

The other girl simply waved at Lacuna.

"And that's Tobi," Kelisha said nervously. "I'm sorry. She has anxiety, so she's not great around new people."

"Wait!" Tobi spoke up suddenly. "I'm not trying to be rude or anything." She looked at Lacuna, a scared expression flickering over her features, before quickly looking at Kelisha. She gestured the other closer to her, saying softly, "You don't have to speak up for me. I'll be ok. I promise."

Kelisha mouthed, "Are you sure?"

Tobi made a weird gesture at Kelisha, one that Kelisha appeared to understand well, nodding in reply.

Lacuna observed their actions pensively.

"I'm glad everyone is getting to know each other!"

Expressions of agreement were exclaimed by both girls, with Lacuna contemplating over Tobi's status in the school.

"I have a question to ask you, Tobi," Lacuna asked monotonously.

"Uh... yes?"

Lacuna plopped down on the blanket next to Tobi. "You have a really interesting hair color. It reminds me of a fairy."

Another flicker of fear came over Tobi's face. "Yeah... I guess it kind of does." She looked down and played with her hair.

As Lacuna was about to question Tobi further, she suddenly felt the presence of someone familiar. She turned around carefully, attempting to not alarm the rest of the group. A few yards away, she saw familiar black hair and dark carnelian eyes. Sonai Adalim.

Now there were two fae in one place.

"Maybe I can kill two birds with one stone?" she thought to herself.

Sonai was coming right to her, with an angered look on her face. But, that wasn't usually the look she gave Lacuna?

Tobi looked in the same direction as Lacuna. This time her expression was that of complete fear, rather than the flickers she had given Lacuna at her questioning.

"Um, I have to go!" Tobi exclaimed nervously, before suddenly getting up and dashing in the direction of the woods.

"Huh? Tobi, what's wrong?" asked Kelisha as she stood up too.

Sonai dashed in a large arc past the picnic blanket in Tobi's direction. When Kelisha saw her, she too became fearful, dashing after them.

An opportunity was presenting itself for Lacuna. She looked towards Ala, who sat perplexed.

"Where's everyone going?"

"I have no idea, but I can go check. You should stay here and protect the food." Satisfied with her answer, Lacuna ran after Sonai.

Ala was left alone on the picnic blanket, confused as per usual. With a defeated sigh, she grabbed a muffin. What was wrong with her friends?

As the four girls ran towards the wood, Tobi shouted, "I'm not going back!" She suddenly became semi-transparent, phasing through the iron gate in panic. Sonai simply soared over the gate, while Lacuna vaulted over after a short climb. Kelisha was unfortunately stuck behind the fence, gazing in awe of the other girl's talents.

Sonai chased Tobi past winding trees, hanging branches and sharp bushes. Lacuna was close behind, at least, originally. Once they were deep into the forest, Sonai transformed into her Feomin form, gaining speed with her increased powers. The shy, false human persona that Tobi took on before, portrayed her as weak. The version of Tobi that Lacuna could see now, semi-transparent, phasing between the two realms, was partially demonstrating her true fae powers. It shocked Lacuna as she took in deep breaths chasing after her original target. She could barely keep up with the two beings from the other side of the Veil.

The scenery rushed past the three girls as they went deeper into the forest. No wonder the cafe had such a large gate blocking it off. Lacuna began to wonder if there were any animals here.

"I'm not going back!" Tobi screamed at Sonai again, an increased sense of desperation in her voice. "I will never again be under the rule of Her Majesty again!"

"You know you don't have a choice! Stop fighting!" Sonai growled. She summoned a magic orb and threw it at a tree near Tobi. The mark it left on the tree was much larger than it was inside of Podim University when Lacuna fought her.

Tobi scrambled away from the blast, nearly tripping before dashing to the right. The angry Feomin continued to give chase. Eventually the three girls found themselves in front of a massive tree. Tobi was flickering more rapidly, stumbling towards the tree.

"Stop resisting Tobi," Sonai stated calmly as she slowly walked towards her. "At this rate you're gonna phase through the Veil. And you know what's waiting for you if that happens."

Tobi backed towards the tree, shaking. She leaned against it heavily with a low groan.

"There's a less painful way back to Melterra if you just stop running from me." She outstretched a hand.

Melterra? Was that what faeries called their realm on the other side of the Veil? Lacuna knew that other faeries who weren't Feomin eventually phased back over, but she had no idea it was painful for them. Exactly how much power was Tobi using to stay within the realm? And at the rate she was flickering, how was she still here?

In fact, why did Tobi try to run at all if the outcome would be the same no matter what?

As Tobi continued to struggle against the will of the realms, Sonai turned her body so that her attention could be on Lacuna as well. "You came at an inconvenient time, Lacuna. You weren't supposed to be here." Her voice lacked its usual taunting nature. "But don't worry, I'll deal with you later." Despite her statement implying a temporary truce, she sends a blast at Lacuna anyways. She sidesteps it easily.

"Is Tobi the reason why you're at Podim?"

Sonai doesn't reply to the question, instead turning all of her attention back to Tobi. The girl was now completely slumped against the tree, breathing heavily and groaning. The flickering was becoming even more persistent, with Tobi nearly disappearing every few seconds.

"Tobi, you don't have to do this to yourself…" Sonai said softly as she approached Tobi again. "The transportation spell is quick and simple. All I need is your consent. You know I can't do the spell without that; I'll be forced to leave you here to painfully phase back. Any guards that find you back home will be a lot harder on you than I am right now." Her voice becomes softer. "In fact, they'll probably petition for your execution, if they aren't already…"

Lacuna didn't know much about faerie customs, no matter how much research she did in the Temple's library. But whatever Tobi was in trouble for couldn't be for simply being here in the human realm.

Sonai continued to approach the flickering fae. Tobi began to stand up, struggling, weakly using the tree as support. Her hair fell over her eyes once again. But it did not hide the small smirk on her face. She murmured something incomprehensible under her breath. Lacuna was confused. Sonai was not.

Wide-eyed, she turned around quickly, Lacuna following her movements. Suddenly a blast of magic shot towards the two girls. Sonai dodged the blast of magic with ease, but Lacuna, who didn't expect it, stumbled a bit while trying to evade it. Upon collecting herself, she turned her attention towards the mysterious attacker, realizing it was Kelisha.

"Stay away from her!" she shouted at the two of them with a staff pointed in their direction. Her quivering form took away from any intimidation her magic had originally caused.

Sonai glares at her with a long animated sigh, claws appearing sharper. She stood with her back directly in front of Tobi. Lacuna backs away from the fight with her hands up, shaking her head, hopefully signaling to Kelisha that Tobi is not her target here.

Kelisha charged forward, sending another magic blast at Sonai.

Stepping out of the way simply, she taunts, "Simple magic blasts aren't gonna be enough to hurt me, witch."

"I know," Kelisha replied snarkily as she began backing away. Her bracelet, which was previously silver, transformed into amethyst color. And Tobi was gone.

"She let herself become a familiar…" Sonai growled through clenched teeth. "The lengths that criminals will go…" She shouted at Kelisha, "Release her now!"

Kelisha holds up her staff again, shaking in a way reminiscent of Tobi's flickering. "I would never hand her over to you!" She keeps her eyes down, not looking Sonai in the eye.

Sonai transforms back into her human form. "You have no idea what she's done. What she's truly done." Her voice is chilled. "She's not just your average run-away faerie."

"I…" Kelisha was hesitant. "I know."

But did she really?

Originally, Lacuna simply *wanted* to understand what this conflict was about. But perhaps she *needed* to understand? This seemed important. It could lead her to the answers she sought after.

"What is going on?"

"What's going on here is none of your business. In fact, you shouldn't be here at all." Her laugh echoes through the forest. "Honestly, why do you want to fight me so badly? I said that I'd deal with you later, didn't I?" She stares down at Lacuna. "So go."

Kelisha continued to back away slowly, fearing what would happen if she turned her sight away from the Feomin to run. It was an agreeable fear to possess, as Sonai threw another fiery magic ball at her. Kelisha created a shield to block it, yet couldn't hold back all of its power, causing her to fall.

"Don't. Move," Sonai growled, low and dangerous.

Even if this situation between Sonai, Kelisha, and Tobi wasn't any of her business, there were two other things that were. Killing Sonai. And figuring out what the Olan was.

Lacuna steps in front of Kelisha. "I'm not going anywhere, Sonai Adalim. I came to Podim to complete a mission." She readies a sword, circling around Sonai. "And your issues with another unruly faerie will stop me from completing that mission."

Sonai follows her movements. "I came here to complete a mission too." The fires behind her eyes burned with a brightness that Lacuna hadn't seen in a while. "Maybe it really is time to end this. I felt sad for you, thinking you were another imprisoned faerie forced into this. But you really are just another brainwashed Arius." She throws a fireball at Lacuna, who reflects it with her shield. As Sonai catches the fire, she transforms back into her faerie form, glowing with a malevolent aura. She creates a wiry, crooked sword from the air and rushes towards Lacuna. The two swords clash against each other, sending subtle waves of energy across the forest.

"At this rate, the witch and the fugitive are gonna get away. I seriously don't have time for this."

"Why does it matter? What did Tobi do? Why are you the one who has to take her back to... Melterra?"

Sonai tries to attack Lacuna's leg, before jumping back. "So we're playing twenty-one questions? Alright then, why on earth are you, as a fae, an Arius?"

"I'm not a monstrous creature like you. And stop avoiding the questions."

"Ouch," Sonai exclaimed, pretending to be hurt. "You know, if I was an older, more powerful Feomin I would instantaneously have your head for a comment like that." She chuckles. "Plus, you can't exactly be the Arius to say that. You're just as... well, maybe even more, monstrous than me."

Lacuna felt enraged at the assumption. She was a proud follower of Marcus Revenali. She vowed to clear every blight on the human realm. Yet somehow she was more monstrous than a Feomin. Disgusting. She spent a lot of time shielding and dodging Sonai's attacks.

It was about time she went on the offensive.

Sonai felt a strange aura form around Lacuna. She prepared a shield instead of a fireball this time. In the blink of an eye, Lacuna released a large blast of energy in Sonai's direction. Trees near the explosion were ripped down, while the leaves on those further away rustled wildly.

A crack formed in her shield.

Once everything calmed down, Sonai slowly turned around to assess the damage. Her regular smiling, taunting persona was gone, replaced with complete shock. She felt drained, *genuinely tired* from the amount of magic she had to use. Against this failure of an Arius?

Lacuna slowly raised her sword. "I won't ask again. What did Tobi do?" She approaches her.

Sonai backs away, cautious and still shocked. Unfortunately, it wasn't cautious enough, as she ungracefully trips over a rock. Lacuna takes the opportunity to lunge onto her, positioning the sword right above her neck. She glares down, demanding an answer. "Make your choices wisely, faerie."

Sonai's shocked expression falls, and she lays there, thinking. The wind rustles the remaining trees, picking up loose dust that wasn't there mere moments ago. Kelisha was definitely long gone by this point, but in the grand scheme of things, that didn't matter.

Not with what Sonai planned to tell Lacuna in a few moments.

Sonai finally breaks away from her thoughts, deciding to answer Lacuna's question. "Tobi is wanted by the royal court for speaking about the Olan, something that no one other than the Queen should know about. Like I said a while ago, not even I really know." She smirks deviously. "But, even though I didn't before, I'm finally starting to understand now."

Lacuna takes her words into consideration as she looks at the ruined section of forest in front of her.

No...

Sonai repeats, slowly, "Tobi's wanted 'cause she knows something that only the queen should know... I'm hunting her for knowing what the Olan is."

Oh god, no...

Sonai smiles a deep, devilish smile. "She's wanted for knowing about your existence."

The words take a while to truly process in Lacuna's head. Perhaps it was partially due to the cognitive dissonance she experienced daily. But once they did, the same shocked expression Sonai had mere moments ago appeared on her face too.

Lacuna and Sonai were more alike than she thought was possible. She was a faerie.

CHAPTER 7

Lacuna finally understood. She didn't want to, but she did. In a way, she was simply trying to avoid the truth this entire time. But why now? She'd seen other Arius use magic before. Powerful magic. So what was it about today that showed her she was... *different?* Was it Sonai's comments? The amount of power she used? Or maybe the methods that other Arius used to get such power–methods that she has never had to use?

Was it that obvious?

Lacuna was no longer on top of Sonai, sitting across from her instead, with her hands over her knees. Sonai continued to lay on the ground, now in human form. Both girls were quiet. They were quiet for a long time.

Sonai eventually sat up, asking, "Do you get it now?"

Lacuna didn't reply.

"Will you finally stop trying to kill me then?"

Lacuna stood up quickly in a display of might. "No. I have a mission to complete."

She had dropped her sword over ten minutes ago.

"As a faerie, do you truly want to kill one of your kin?" She stared up at her. "Because an organization created for killing *us*, kidnapped and brainwashed you? You're gonna let them do that to you?"

"There is no us. And I was not kidnapped nor brainwashed."

Sonai got up with as much might as Lacuna had moments ago. "Then why am I not dead yet?"

Lacuna had no reply. Again.

"Every time I mention the Olan, you stop fighting. You have this big important mission to complete? Then why do you stop fighting? It's like your failing on purpose."

"I..."

"It's like this is the first time you've ever done a mission like this before."

"It is."

Sonai looked at her dumbfounded. "Huh?"

"This is my very first official mission."

Sonai pinched the bridge of her nose. "That's impossible."

Lacuna shook her head. "I have fought fae before in Revenali. But this is my first mission as an Arius."

Sonai walked around the area, staring at her dumbfounded. "Who would send an inexperienced Arius after *me*? Do you know how many of you assassins I've had to fight off in my life?"

Even if Sonai knew about Revenali and its Arius, she doubted the possibility of her knowing about the Oracle. Lacuna refused to mention them.

"No matter how hard you try, you would never be able to kill me the way you are now. Not even with how…" she gestured to the destroyed trees, "crazy your powers are. And I don't think you're supposed to know what the concept of the Olan is, assuming that it really is you."

Lacuna shook her head. "From what I've been told, most practitioners of magic have heard of the Olan, but no one really understands it as a concept. And yet…" Her expression was dejected; words trailed off into a murmur. "I managed to attain some sense of understanding, and now the only being that could lead me to the answers I seek is one that I have to kill."

"Mmm hmm, I guess we have a lot to talk about then. But if you want answers, we should probably go somewhere more… comfortable…" She looked around at the destroyed trees again, looking towards the cafe. "And less out in the open." She sighed, placing her hands on her hips. "I really don't have time for this. Honestly, if I didn't feel so bad for you, you would've been gone already! And now I know you're kinda related to my own mission…" She lets her hands fall to her sides with another sigh. "I don't want to kill you anymore. Anyways, meet me in dorm room 135 B at 5:30. I'll go and confirm the entry request right now." Sonai began to walk away in the direction opposite to where they came from, exclaiming, "And you should probably check on Ala. Tobi and the witch didn't, most likely."

Upon getting back to the cafe, it turned out that Sonai was right. Tobi and Kelisha never came back, and Ala had been left all alone to enjoy her meal. Lacuna apologizes, then lies that Tobi had let go of an assignment on accident, and it had flown towards the forest. Coincidently, Tobi really had been working on something before she ran, but it was unlikely anything really flew into the woods. But luckily for her, Ala hadn't been paying attention.

"Me and Kelisha were simply trying to help her," Lacuna stated montonely.

"So, is that why Sonai came out of nowhere?" Ala questioned.

"Yes!" She surmised. "And again, I'm sorry about this situation. By the time Tobi finally got the paper back, it was time for her to attend her next class."

"I understand," Ala whined. A moment later, she suddenly perked up. "Actually, there's another time that we can all hang out together! Delilah, she's a friend of mine, and her birthday is coming up! She's gonna have a party at the bowling alley downtown."

Lacuna looked at her placidly, with an expression that Ala interpreted as meaning something else.

"Oh, it's a small party. Definitely not one of those college parties, if you get what I mean." She pauses, a small smile forming on her lips. "Well, actually… Delilah…" She doesn't actually finish the sentence, giggling at a suppressed joke that only she could understand. "But of course, it's nothing crazy!"

Lacuna recalled her behavior in the cafeteria a few days ago, asking if she was interested in Sonai. After finally looking up the meaning, Lacuna concluded that the answer was *"definitely not!"* She still had yet to audibly tell Ala this, but why would she even suggest such a thing in the first place? Overall, Ala seemed to find her vague behavior hilarious, even if Lacuna did not.

"I'm gonna go and ask Delilah if it's ok for you to come, since I saw her walk by like two seconds ago. She wanted all guests to RSVP. I'll text you if she says yes!" Ala began to run away.

"But I don't have your phone number!" Lacuna yelled after her.

"Oh yeah! I forgot." She rushed back over, taking Lacuna's phone, quickly putting her number in and Lacuna's number into her own. She then runs again, nearly bumping into a group of people.

They whisper comments about Ala antics that are incoherent to Lacuna's ears, but she could clearly hear their laughter and statements of agreement. Friendly discussions about unknown topics. Even if she could understand what they were talking about, it was likely she currently lacked the type of people needed to discuss said topic with. She found herself staring at the group, then staring at the new number in her phone. Could she ever gain people like that in her life?

Lacuna realized that it was currently 2:15 P.M. After her final few classes, there would be a lot she needed to prepare for. She was inching closer to the truth.

At 4:30, Lacuna sat in her dorm room, sharpening her sword. Next to her was a pile of laundry. It had been sitting on the bed for days. Luckily, a few pieces of clothing in the pile would finally leave its dejected mass. After quickly checking the vitality of her magic, she shifted through the clothes, looking for an outfit that would be good in a potential fight. Not too tight, but not too loose. Strong, yet not too intimidating. Maybe something with denim?

She eventually settled on a plain turtleneck without sleeves, protecting her arms with a jacket similar in color to her black jeans. At exactly 5:30 P.M, Lacuna stood in front of room 135 B. The entry process didn't take long at all as the lady sitting by the front desk handed her a guest pass, greeting her with her full name. But, did Lacuna ever tell Sonai her full name directly?

Regardless, from outside the room, she could hear low music coming from within. It sounded like a strange mix between rock and roll, and an orchestra? She knocks, hearing both the music stop and what should be the room's sole occupant trip as she curses, "Myco, move!"

Lacuna waited for a while, checking her phone before the door slowly opened. It's Sonai, of course, but she looked… different. Her curly hair was up in a high ponytail, held together by a red band. The color matched the tank top she wore above black leggings, which Lacuna also noticed accentuated the slight muscled curviness of her arms—and her hips.

They both stared at one another for a long moment. Sonai blinked every so often. Lacuna did not.

"What're you dressed so fancy for?" Sonai asked, tilting her head.

"This is fancy?" questioned Lacuna as she looked down at her plainly colored clothing.

"Anyways," Sonai stated with a huff. "Stop staring at me and come in already." She beckoned Lacuna inside before walking away from the door.

Lacuna carefully followed her, taking into account that all of the dorms in building B were single student rooms. They were also incredibly expensive, built like small apartments, which is why the Oracle didn't register for Lacuna to be in one herself, even despite the increased effectiveness it would've had on her mission. She wouldn't have to be so careful when Ala was present if she was in one.

Lacuna stood in the entrance way, near the small kitchen, scanning the area for any strange wires or tiles.

"Girl, it's not booby trapped." Sonai stated with an apathetic voice, glaring at her from the couch.

Lacuna replied, "I see…" looking between Sonai and the couch, before treading towards it. She sat down with a little more trust than before.

Sonai looked down at Lacuna with a breathy smile before walking over to the kitchen. She returns shortly with two drinks in her hand, soda and a bottle of water. She immediately hands Lacuna the water.

"You never asked me what I wanted to drink?" Lacuna stated as she took it. She didn't take off the cap.

"Yeah… but you seem like the type who would only drink water." Sonai took a sip of her soda. "But if you want, I could get you something else."

"No need. I like water." She still hadn't opened it.

"You also seem like the type of person to drink black coffee." Sonai put the soda down on the coffee table.

"Hmm." She continued to stare at the water.

Both girls sat in silence for a moment, as they usually do.

Abruptly, Sonai took the water from Lacuna's hand and downed half the bottle. "It's not poisoned."

Lacuna hums, taking a sip from the bottle. Yep, normal water.

Sonai slumped down next to her with a sigh. "You know, when I said that I don't really know who the Olan is, I was serious. I mean, it's probably you, but I wouldn't know for sure." She turns to look at Lacuna. "I actually had some trouble against you back in the woods today. Based on that alone, you're obviously pretty strong."

"Am I really?" she asked, looking down at her hands. "I'm not sure if my powers could truly serve as proof of me being a faerie. There are a lot of Arius with strong magic powers"

"Example?"

"The leader. And I've never heard of her using a weapon to harness her powers."

"Either way, those are definitely stolen from some poor faerie."

"Proof?"

"Just a hunch." She slumps further against the couch.

Lacuna hummed as she finished her water. "Uh huh…"

"But, over the years I've learned that the power systems of Arius are based on how many fae they've defeated. So the stronger they are, the more magic power they can take." She sits up straight. "I've fought plenty of Arius that don't have powers. Based on the fact that you've mostly seen Arius with power, you only hang around powerful, important people, right?"

Ignoring Sonai's claim, Lacuna asked, "You have fought other Arius before?"

"I'm what you humans call a *Feomin* right? Of course I—" Her facial expression twists. "Ha… you humans…"

"Well, even if I am half fae, I'm still half human."

"Nah. It's more like you're fully human and fully fae."

"That doesn't make sense."

"It makes plenty of sense."

"If we are to conclude that I had one human parent and one faerie parent, then that makes me—"

"Had?"

Lacuna nods. "Or at least that's what they've told me."

"Who?"

"I refuse to say."

"Ok then." Sonai rolls her eyes. "Anyways, let's get back to the topic at hand. You don't think you're a faerie even though you're definitely a faerie."

"I am simply not fully convinced."

"Yeah, but even if we ignore your powers for a second, you've looked me in the eye multiple times while I was in my real form."

"Pardon?"

"Oh my god?" Sonai puts her hands on top of her head as she laughs. "There's no way… you just can't be real."

"What are you talking about?"

"What are you talking about?"

Sonai spoke with a mocking tone. "Has anyone in the amazing Arius organization ever told you that humans can't look most of us fae in the eye?"

Lacuna shook her head. "Why would that be a problem?"

"Well, if someone like that witch Tobi was with—"

"Her name was Kelisha."

"Yeah yeah, whatever. If a human like her were to look me in the eye, then she would start bleeding from her orifices. But she could probably survive with some quick medical attention." She seemed disappointed. "If she looked at the queen though…" Sonai made a chopping motion at her neck.

Lacuna recalled their battle in the bathroom a few weeks ago. The way in which Sonai's blazing red irises glared down at her, like they were trying to bore into her soul. But they couldn't. For a non-human being like herself, they were completely harmless.

"Ok…" Lacuna's facial expression began to match Sonai's. "But that still doesn't make any sense?"

"How?"

"If I'm part fae, then how come humans can look at my eyes?"

"Maybe the human part of you cancels out that type of power in some way. Plus, I can only harm humans with my eyes in my real form. My eyes are completely harmless right now."

Lacuna recalled seeing Kelisha look at Sonai just fine in her human form. But the second she switched, her eyes were averted instantly. Why didn't she take note of this?

They say that eyes are the windows to the soul. And the souls of fae are just as complex and twisted as themselves.

"But now the plot thickens…" Sonai pondered with a fist gently against her mouth. Could a faerie like Sonai really convince Lacuna that her first eighteen years of living were truly a lie? Would she allow herself to be convinced so easily?

"Why would the organization responsible for the deaths of thousands of fae send out an inexperienced Arius who doesn't even know how to avoid being harmed by fae?"

"I know plenty of ways to avoid being harmed," Lacuna retorted.

"No you don't."

"Yes I do. The quickest way to kill a faerie is to–"

"You're not supposed to take food from faeries. It creates contracts."

Lacuna paused.

"And you were drinking that water up, girl." Sonai smirked from behind her hand. "Not even other fae take food from one another without reason."

Lacuna gulped. "Does this mean I'm in a contract with you now?"

"It depends. Anyways, after you looked me in the eye and took food from me with no qualms, it solidified for me that you had to be a kidnapped faerie. You know nothing."

Lacuna let the statement settle in. She sat there for a long time.

"Damn…" Lacuna covered her eyes.

"Mmm hmm." Sonai finished the rest of her soda nonchalantly, leaning back as she watched Lacuna.

She felt like a child in the process of being reprimanded by parents. Repeatedly telling the one who questioned her current state of being that she just *didn't know*. But she did know. It was like she touched something that no one directly told her she *couldn't* touch, but always had a feeling in the back of her mind that she wasn't supposed to touch it anyway. She ignored that feeling for so many years, and now the degrading voice of reason, encapsulated by a Feomin girl, was finally here to punish her.

"Then…" Lacuna thought back to Revenali. It's salted white buildings, citizens dressed ready to kill faeries. To kill her? But they didn't. Did they know? Did the Oracle—oh—they definitely knew. But why would they—they gave her a home? Chocolate after battle training. Dumb jokes. Whoever her real parents were didn't want her, right? But if they did then…

"Then…" Lacuna's voice quivered. "What am I supposed to do?"

Sonai placed the empty can on the table. "Well, that's for you to—"

"No."

Sonai looked at her bewildered, slightly angered.

"I can't just leave Revenali. They do not leave sudden disappearances alone." Lacuna shot up, only a few remnants of her previous shakiness remained. "My mission is still to eliminate you. Even if I believe what you've told me here today."

"So what? You're just gonna kill one of your kin, then go back and get surrounded by more people that want to kill you? What's with this…what's the word?" She pauses to think, "…uh, cognitive dissonance, you got going on here?"

Lacuna doesn't reply.

Sonai gets up and stands directly in front of her. "Look, even if you don't believe me or trust me completely, I trust you." She crouches down on one knee and takes both of Lacuna's hands.

Lacuna's face twists in confusion. She doesn't need Sonai to trust her. Yet there was another emotion bubbling underneath.

"You are a faerie. One of us. And it is my mission as a fae of the royal court to find my captured kin and rescue them. Not harm them. So if you are, truly are, a long lost faerie of Melterra, then I will not harm you. There's no reason for you to keep trying to harm me. You're safe."

She looked down at her hand, the pressure of Sonai's grip allowed her to feel her heartbeat. It was steady, like the clicking of a clock. With a deep, shaky and unsure breath, Lacuna replied, "Ok..."

"And even if you don't want to tell me more about the oh-so mysterious island you come from or who sent you, I need to know why you want to know about the Olan so badly."

"Is it not obvious?"

"Ehh, kinda? Not completely."

"By understand what being the Olan is, I might be able to figure out who my family was."

CHAPTER 8

While Sonai looked around the kitchen for more sodas, Lacuna remained seated on the couch, thinking deeply. A TV show played in the background, something involving baking, but Lacuna wasn't paying attention. Stuck in her own mind, she thought about the Oracle. Their mysterious sayings and odd habits. The way in which their masked eyes never truly looked at her, hiding nearly all of their expressions. Why did they take her?

A half-opened door somewhere in the dorm cracked open further.

Suddenly, Lacuna felt a strange, ticklish texture brush against her ankle. She jumped onto the couch, looking down at the spot. Peering up at her was a large furry creature which glared at her in contemplation. After a few seconds, its mouth opened, silently screaming at her.

As Sonai came back with another soda, she called out to the animal excitedly. "My baby!" She placed her soda on the coffee table and picked the animal, which Lacuna now realized was supposed to be a cat, up into her arms. She smoothed over its dense patch-colored fur lovingly. It purred as it nuzzled into the crook of her neck.

"Where did it come from?" Lacuna stammered from her perch on the couch.

"He lives here with me."

"I'm not sure if animals are allowed in the dorms. But it seems unlikely."

"Technically they're not." A flash of sadness came across Sonai's face. "But the RA of building B has a couple secrets of her own that she's hiding, so I don't have much to worry about." As she continued to pet the cat, she asked Lacuna, "Do you want to hold him? He seems to like you."

Lacuna shook her head with her hand up. "I don't know how to hold a cat."

"I'll show you if you stop standing on my couch," Sonai replied plainly, nuzzling him more.

Lacuna slowly slid back into a seating position, arms held directly in front of her body expectantly; fists clenched tightly. She trusted herself to fight unknown fae and learn magic, but petting a cat? There were few cats in Revenali, and none of them were around the Oracle's temple. She could only learn about them through books.

Sonai gently set the cat in her lap. He sniffed Lacuna's hand before rubbing against it.

"You can pet him now."

Lacuna lowered her hand slowly over his back, patting the middle.

"Uh uh, not like that!" She shook her head, taking Lacuna's hand and leading it over the cat's fur. "Like this."

Letting Sonai's hand lead her own, she examined the cat with slight puzzlement. "I think he's overweight."

Sonai sighed, "Yeah. I know. Myco likes his wet food a lot."

"I can see that quite clearly."

Myco looked up at Lacuna and opened his mouth. No sound resounded from the small mouth that was more similar to the void than an oral cavity.

Lacuna quickly pulled her hand away. "Is he trying to bite me?"

"Nah. He's trying to meow. But he can't." Sonai's tone became somber as she sat down next to Lacuna. "He has no vocal cords."

Lacuna looked at Sonai in disbelief, then back at Myco, gently setting her hand on his back. Sonai silently took Myco from her lap, holding up one of his paws. She gently pushed down on the top of his paw pad.

No claws.

"I'm guessing when he tried to meow you saw…"

Lacuna nodded, Sonai no longer having to finish the sentence. She had seen the void.

No fangs.

"Did you—"

"Never. I would never."

Lacuna didn't particularly care about animals. There were so few on Revenali, and they were never in places that she was allowed to visit anyway. Yet still, for a person to defang, declaw, and take the vocal cords of an animal was—cruel—beyond cruel.

"How did he become like this?"

Sonai shrugged. "I don't really know. He was like this when I found him a few years ago."

Sonai recalled that day when she was thirteen years old, walking home from school. At the time, this home of hers was a treehouse deep in the woods; hidden from human eyes. It had been given to her by an old acquaintance, one she met long ago in the beginning of her journey in the human realm. One who gave her endless opportunities, happiness, and a name. But that was a story for another time.

Sonai walked along a dusty dirt path, faintly visible through the efforts of her own feet. Soon after, she came across an animal.

White fur reflected the thin lines of sun coming through the canopy of trees. The animal laid curled up against the emerald grass, breathing heavily and shaking. To one with more spatial awareness, it was obviously hurt.

"Aww, a kitten!" Young Sonai exclaimed, originally ignorant to the cat's pain. She simply thought it was cold. She leaned down to pet it—what would've been a dangerous mistake had the cat been healthy. He lunged upward at the unknown guest, hackles raised. Yet he couldn't protect himself properly. The parts of his paws where nails should be were bloodied. And he was tired. Deathly tired. As quickly as he got up, the small fearful animal fell back down. He made an attempt at producing sound, but the action caused his eyes to water.

Sonai kneeled on the ground, finally realizing the obvious. She approached him slowly, although trying to prevent scaring him didn't really matter. He was already scared of her. And he couldn't run. She scooped the cat into her arms and analyzed his paws. Her assumption was correct. No claws.

He attempted to bite her hand weakly, notifying Sonai of another issue. Gently holding open his mouth, she looked into the void. Small scars lined his gums in a deliberate pattern. They appeared fresh.

"Aww, you poor thing…" Sonai whispered, petting the cat slowly. He continued to shake, looking directly into her eyes. He flinched, sensing that his visitor wasn't like other beings within his world. He was lucky that eyes from the Otherside couldn't affect animals in the way that affected humans. It seemed to be one of the only lucky things he had going for him. Sonai picked up the cat, smiling, and continued walking. From that day forward, she kept Myco with her. There was no reason for a fae like her to keep a cat as injured as he was in her treehouse. But, Myco was another being who could stay with her and fill the vacancy that Ms. Adalim had left behind.

Hearing the story, Lacuna felt conflicted. An act like that appeared too affectionate for someone like Sonai. Or rather, that's what she believed from her perspective. Either way, while the gesture was kind at face value, a cat missing so many vital parts of its body would only be unhappy.

"Why did you leave him alive?" Lacuna questioned. "Would it not have been easier to just end his suffering?"

"He was cute, so I kept him," Sonai stated simply, continuing to pet Myco.

"That's somewhat cruel, isn't it?"

"I don't need an Arius to tell me what's cruel or not. And look at him." She gestured to Myco's purring form. "He's happy."

Despite his purring, Lacuna didn't entirely agree. "Does he just sit in your dorm all day, every day?"

"Yeah, but it's like that for most cats, ain't it?"

Lacuna contemplated the statement for a moment. She thought of some of the books she'd read before. Some cats walked around outdoors, conversing with other cats in their incomprehensible language. Meows and hisses, things that Myco could no longer do. Cats played with toys and scratched at posts. Myco had no claws. Cats chased small creatures and ate fish, but Myco had no fangs. The amount of things he could do within his short cat life was cut by around eighty percent.

She found it hard to believe he could truly be happy. Or healthy.

Yet a discussion regarding Myco's well-being wasn't what Lacuna had come here to do. In all honesty, she could care less about the cat. It was mostly Sonai's methods that she wanted to question so badly. To keep a suffering creature alive, even while having the ability to stop it in a quick and painless way, and simply because she found him cute was borderline inhuman. Yet, Lacuna knew of humans who did the same thing all the time. Letting pets and even human loved ones suffer because of their relationship, inevitably treating them like an inanimate piece of property.

So was humanity really the determinant of cruelty? And if so, then how different was a human like herself from a faerie like Sonai?

Consequently, Lacuna learned a lot about the fae from today's conversation.

Sonai placed Myco back on the floor. He pranced back towards the bathroom, preparing to take a nap. Lacuna looked at the window and the darkness of evening looked back at her.

"It's getting late." She stood up and stretched, preparing to follow in Myco's footsteps and make her way towards the door. "Have a good evening."

"Woah, what'chu in such a hurry for? I haven't told you what I was gonna do about Tobi yet."

Lacuna looked down at her. "And that is?"

Yet a discussion regarding Myco's well-being wasn't what Lacuna had come here to do. In all honesty, she could care less about the cat. It was mostly Sonai's methods that she wanted to question so badly. To keep a suffering creature alive, even while having the ability to stop it in a quick and painless way, and simply because she found him cute was borderline inhuman. Yet, Lacuna knew of humans who did the same thing all the time. Letting pets and even human loved ones suffer because of their relationship, inevitably treating them like an inanimate piece of property.

So was humanity really the determinant of cruelty? And if so, then how different was a human like herself from a faerie like Sonai?

Consequently, Lacuna learned a lot about the fae from today's conversation.

Sonai placed Myco back on the floor. He pranced back towards the bathroom, preparing to take a nap. Lacuna looked at the window and the darkness of evening looked back at her.

"It's getting late." She stood up and stretched, preparing to follow in Myco's footsteps and make her way towards the door. "Have a good evening."

"Woah, what'chu in such a hurry for? I haven't told you what I was gonna do about Tobi yet."

Lacuna looked down at her. "And that is?"

"We have to find Tobi, save her from that witch, and convince her to tell us the secret of the Olan." Sonai slouched into the couch for the second time that evening. "But… I'm not sure how to do it though."

"I don't think she needs saving from Kelisha. The two of them are friends, I believe." Lacuna felt her phone vibrate in her pocket.

Sonai clicked her tongue. "Becoming the familiar of a witch is all bad news. They're just so exploitative…"

As Sonai began to rant, Lacuna looked down at the text message recently sent to her.

Ala: Hey it's Ala. Deliah told me you could come!!! :)

Lacuna had an idea.

Lacuna: Thank you. Would you mind if I asked two questions?

Ala: Go ahead

Lacuna: Firstly, I wish to know if it is ok for me to bring another person to the party? Secondly, I wish to know if Tobi is going to be there?

Ala: You're so formal even while texting wow. Also, it's a yes to both questions!! See you on October 23 :)

Ala: Wait, who are you bringing?

Lacuna: Sonai Adalim.

Ala: Ohhhhhh your girlfriend ;)

Lacuna: Pardon?

Ala: ;)

Lacuna: Ala, what is the meaning of this?

Ala: ;)

Ala: See you both on the 23rd!!

Lacuna: Ala?

Lacuna: Ala? Please respond.

Ala didn't reply after that.

"Why do you look so distressed?" Sonai asked from the couch.

Lacuna shook her head. "Ala was acting nonsensical. But I actually have good news. Tobi will be at the party of Ala's friend, Delillah, and she has allowed the both of us to attend."

Sonai clicks her tongue. "Of course she's gonna hide in plain sight like that…"

"Now why do you look so distressed?"

She mumbles, "I hate parties…"

"I assumed you would love parties."

Sonai giggled. "You assume a lot of things about me."

Between fae and humans, the beings on both sides of the Veil often assumed a lot of things about one another. And in order to turn these assumptions from theories into truths, the Arius of Revenali researched diligently. As evening settled in Podim, Ohio, late afternoon was just beginning in Revenali.

What was told to the public during the Somnium Conference was simply a sneak peak at what was to come. The machine was being developed in an underground lab, accessible to only the most elite of Arius. Luckily for him, Jordan managed to become one of such Arius through his role in Morana's unit. The area consisted of many long, dark hallways that lead towards a large main room. Jordan discussed formalities with one of the researchers to the left of a small cage. Inside was a pixie, struggling desperately against the bars. A researcher to the right of the cage held a small, taser like object. And looking down at all four of the figures from a large platform was Morana Rune.

"Prepare the device!" she yelled from her imposing position.

The researcher on the right held up the machine clicking a couple buttons on the side. Jordan and the other researcher backed away from the cage. The pixie became more erratic in its movements, banging against the metal a few more times before huddling in a corner. It began to turn transparent.

"Fae shifting sequence initiated. Shall we proceed?" announced the researcher next to Jordan.

"Yes!" Morana declared. "Administer negation."

An electric purple glow was emitted from the device instantly. The researcher holding it strode towards the cage, thrusting it at the pixie. The fae twitched rapidly, turning more opaque as the seconds went by. Upon entering their side Veil fully, it skittered towards the other end of the cage, exhausted.

Jordan applauded. "Which would you say is more painful for the fae? Phasing back through naturally or touching the device?" Jordan shouted to Morana.

"I was informed that they should be around the same," she shouted back with the same level of volume. "You know, you should come up here so we can discuss more professionally." She laughed, the sound echoing throughout the room. "We don't have't keep yelling at each other."

Upon climbing the stairs and reaching Morana's location, Jordan asked, "How is this all possible?"

"In all honesty, I'm not entirely sure." Morana began walking down one of the second-floor hallways. Jordan followed behind her silently. "I think it has something to do with turning their own magic against themselves, but I'm not the one in charge of knowing the specifics." She turned around to face him once they entered a smaller room.

"Hmm?" Jordan hummed in question.

"The Oracle is the main operator in all of this."

"I see…" Following along, Jordan asked, "Does the device have a name yet?"

"As of right now, the facility wishes to keep the name unknown while the device is still in its infancy."

"I see…" Jordan repeated.

Morana cleared her throat. "By the way, did you see my message?"

"Of course. And there's no need to worry, I'll be handling the situation with group 1B starting Wednesday."

"Excellent," Morana stated simply. "However, I believe it would be best if you headed into Sweden soon after this meeting. The situation seems dire."

Jordan pinched the bridge of his nose. "Yes, I know." He sighed. "Thirty-five civilian casualties in total as of yesterday. It's an extreme number for a situation that started merely a month ago."

Morana nodded.

He dropped his hand, putting them into his pockets. "That's why I want to be prepared."

"Understandable. I wish you the best of luck."

"Thank you, High Arius Rune."

For a while longer, Jordan spoke with Morana about the various events happening in and outside of Revenali. Upon exiting the facility, located on a small hill away from the town square, he walked towards the Western Portal gate. Past shops and conversations, the glint of sword hilts and the sea's surface illuminated his path towards the next battle.

Strolling along, he came across one of the island's academies; yet a more accurate term for them would be barracks. To be a Revenalian citizen was to be a warrior. No matter the age or gender. The only possible excluding factor was disability, which wasn't often. Various roles could be given to an Arius, from physical assassinations to informant studies. Jordan looked towards the courtyard, observing as the children spared against one another with foam swords. Would they be as excited as he was once the real thing was bestowed upon them?

Jordan continued to reminisce about his school days. Fights, magic troubles, brawls for status. Albeit childish pursuits, they eventually morphed into motivation; all for the good of the earth.

He was excited to see the development of the new, currently unnamed device. Having direct control over when fae could come and go through the Veil would significantly increase Revenali's impact on the world. The Veil itself was one the only thing stopping Revenali from marching into the fae realm directly. Past its foggy metaphorical walls, the magic and fae that could reside on the other side were simply too unknown and dangerous. Small missions to send scouts into the realm had proved unsuccessful in the past, with entire units going MIA a few hours after entry.

Not one had ever come back out.

Unfortunately for Jordan Mitchels, he and a few of his associates may become one of these units soon. Throughout the month, before the Somnium conference, various meetings with the Oracle and Morana Rune were held in secret. The Red Cap incident in Sweden had been revealed to involve a large Tear in the Veil. Essentially, a portal between the realms was forcibly ripped open. Despite the large number of fae coming through the Tear, it was currently unknown whether or not it was made by such fae. In fact, Morana suspected that a witch was involved in its creation. Either way, the Oracle wanted to use the Tear as a means of entry into the fae realm. It was currently Revenali's safest option, as ironic as it sounded.

Only faeries, and those directly involved with faeries in a contractual way, could open Tears in the Veil. Regular humans and the dictatorial Arius of Revenali could not. Previous ways of entry involved forcing fae to create Tears, often awakening malevolent forms and powers that were previously docile.

The carnage in these situations was reminiscent of crushed pomegranates. And thus, it was up to Jordan to lead a team away from the possibility of human bloodshed. Towards hope.

Towards the future.

CHAPTER 9

A s Lacuna stood in front of the rustic bowling alley, the cool autumn breeze blew leaves around its exterior. Like tornados depicted in picture books, their unusual curving, twirling, spinning in one place had intrigued Lacuna as a child. It was rare that she saw a sight like this. The longer she traveled in Podim, the more she compared the climate to Revenali's. The seasons changed rapidly here. In fact, a small flurry of snow landed a few days ago, and although its time frame was short, it nonetheless signified the arrival of winter. A season that also never lands in Revenali.

However, in the current moment, all that Lacuna could question was whether or not the spinning of the leaves was due to the wind, or if small faeries were being embraced by their dance. But no matter how hard she strained her ears to listen for small giggles, she heard nothing but the wind. Maybe they weren't happy?

If so, then they were not the only fae alone in their unhappiness. Sonai shivered as she pulled her jacket closer to her body. Her normally fiery attitude had also been replaced by the wind, perhaps attempting to swirl its way back home to Myco. The two girls didn't arrive together, not wanting to bring attention to themselves in case Tobi was nearby. Their sneaking consisted of hiding in plain sight. Or rather, in a fanciful sight, since the bright red blouse that Sonai decided to wear today definitely stood out. Lacuna was in what she considered more sensible clothing. It was similar to what she wore in Sonai's room a week ago, but without the jacket. Last she checked, the temperature outside was nearly sixty degrees, and it felt that way too.

"You look nice today," Lacuna said to the shivering girl, who had just now walked up to her.

Sonai grunted. "Let's get inside already. It's freezing out here." She rubbed her arms, despite them being underneath her jacket's long sleeves, and murmured, "Weather apps are so inaccurate."

Upon entering the building, the two were bombarded by the striking beats of pop music, the smell of nachos, and sight of glowing screens under dim lighting. The small, decrepit bowling alley was crammed with people.

"Is it usually like this?" questioned Sonai as she surveyed the room. A bowling ball nearby slammed against the wooden bowling lane, forcefully. Two people holding canned beers walked past, laughing loudly at jokes that were incoherent to the two girls. Sonai pushed herself closer to Lacuna.

"I'm not sure. I have never been here before," Lacuna replied, not acknowledging Sonai's weight against her side. She looked around while walking towards the shoe station. "I think I recognize a few of these people from school."

Sonai muttered, "Uh huh…Delilah must be pretty popular then."

Nearby, a man roared. "Strike!"

His friends burst into loud chuckles and screams, with one girl in the group yelling, "Nah, no way! He cheated!" Retorts were thrown her way; the cacophony of their personal party reverberated through the bowling alley.

Despite the noise, the group definitely wasn't the loudest in the building that evening, albeit, they were the closest to the two girls. Sonai shuffled even closer to Lacuna at the sound.

"You are oddly clingy today, Sonai. Are you alright?"

It took a second for Sonai to reply, silently snarling towards the people yelling and laughing. "Hmm, oh? I'll be fine in a little bit."

Although not satisfied with her answer, Lacuna led the both of them to the long line at the shoe station. In the middle of their wait, Lacuna finally spotted Ala, who was coming towards the station from the back of the bowling alley. It seemed like she had emerged from one of the booths. Along with her was a light-skinned woman wearing a sparkly, short dress. It reflected the glaring lights of the alley like a disco ball, nearly blinding Lacuna as was about to wave hello.

"That must be the birthday girl," Sonai stated, glaring beneath her eyelashes. The way in which she currently pressed herself against Lacuna made her appear smaller, which shouldn't be possible in Lacuna's opinion. They were around the same height.

"Are you completely sure you're alright, Sonai?"

"I already answered that question!" she snapped. But she still didn't look up towards her.

Lacuna tilted her head to try and get a better look at Sonai's face. In order to avoid rousing more anger from her, she said, "If you say so…"

Ala was saying something to Delilah that couldn't be heard through the harsh sounds of the alley. She pointed in the direction of the small arcade, near the entryway. Upon turning to look at it herself, Ala finally spotted the two girls, excitedly running over to greet them.

"Hey guys!" she smiled.

"Good afternoon, Ala."

"Hey…"

Ala led the two towards a booth in the far back of the building. Directly nearby appeared to be the designated party room, a small room separated from the rest of the area by glass doors. Inside, the lighting was dim and warm, greatly contrasting with the kaleidoscope lighting near the bowling lanes. The low buzzing sound of a fan could also be heard from outside the room. It was evidently too small for the various guests in the bowling alley. However, a couple people were inside, surrounded by a few balloons and streamers. There was also a nicely sized chocolate cake, sitting on top of a folding table.

Ala gestured around the area. "So this is where we're all gonna sit. If you're hungry, you don't have to order pizza 'cause Jason and Delilah already did."

Speaking of Deliliah, the woman herself walked over to the booth just as Lacuna and Sonai sat down. "Hey y'all! Thanks for coming! I'm Deliliah."

"It is our pleasure," Lacuna said, looking up at her with a slight nod. "Happy Birthday Delilah. And I am Lacuna."

Delilah paused for a split second at the formal tone of Lacuna's voice. "Thanks Lacuna, and it's nice to meet you!"

She then looked at Sonai. Her greeting was simple and she waved with no introduction. "Hey."

Ala spoke up, standing next to Delilah. "I was just about to go beat Delilah at air hockey. Did either of you want to go to the arcade with us?"

Lacuna and Sonai shook their heads. Delilah gave Ala an animated glare, tilting her eyebrows.

"Ok then we'll see you later!"

"So you think you can beat me? You better watch yourself!" Delilah remarked sarcastically.

As the two girls walked away, Lacuna focused her attention on Sonai, who was aimlessly scrolling on her phone, still cowering against her in the form of nonchalant slumping. She wasn't entirely sure if it was a conscious effort, even despite how jarring of an action it was for the normally high-spirited Feomin.

"Why are you acting this way today? I understand that you don't like parties, but it's like you're making an attempt to dissociate from reality."

"There's no way Tobi's gonna be at this party," Sonai stated, ignoring the question.

"Sonai, while I can agree in some aspects, that doesn't have anything to do with my question." She looked her in the eye, throwing an arm over Sonai's shoulder. "What is wrong with you?"

"Wow, ok. Kinda' pushy today aren't we..." Sonai murmured. She finally put her phone down.

"I'm only being more forceful because you're acting strangely today. It's not like you to cling onto me like this."

"Mmm hmm..." Sonai pushed herself off of Lacuna, scooting all the way to the other side of the booth in an instant.

A strange emptiness materialized within her as Sonai's warmth left her side. Had she made her even more uncomfortable?

"I'm sorry. You don't have to tell me what's wrong if you don't want to."

Sonai let out a deep sigh. "There's no one here."

"What do you mean? We are surrounded by people."

"We're surrounded by humans. There aren't any fae around here." She grumbles, "That's rare."

Lacuna tilts her head, questioning the statement.

Sonai sighs again. "No matter where we are, fae are always there. Either on this side of the Veil, directly on the Veil, or in Melterra. When they're here, they look like you and me. When they are on the Veil directly, they appear see-through, as..." She does jazz hands without any flare. "Apparitions." Her attempted goofiness is short-lived. "But if we don't want to look like that, we can use magic. Either way, we simply appear in flashes to humans. But I can use Veil Sight to see other fae nearby."

"So you have the ability to see fae along on the Veil?"

"Yep. I heard that a lot of witches can too."

"Do you spend a lot of time on the Veil yourself?"

Sonai paused for a second. "Ehh... every once and a while. But I don't have any real reason to. It's not just fae here and on the Veil that I can't see; Veil Sight lets me see all the way into Melterra.

"Huh?"

"Let me explain how it works on fae in Melterra." She readjusts her sleeves. "From this side, we appear in odd ways. Through dreams, strange auras, and messages that would be unusual to humans... sometimes we can be seen in the in-between places..."

"Are you referring to liminal spaces?" Lacuna asks, once again interrupting her.

"I guess so? All in all, the point of me telling you this is that..." She searches around the bowling alley one last time, "No matter how hard I try, I can't sense any other fae here." She rubs her arms, slightly shivering like she was earlier. "There's always at least one faerie who's decided to make their territory a place like this. There's tons of energy here, so someone should be around. But right now, there's no one. I'm alone here, surrounded by humans."

Before Lacuna could reply, Ala had returned. "Did you guys want anything to drink?" she asked immediately. "Delilah went to go get drinks, and I'm gonna help carry them. If you want anything with alcohol in it, Jason will order it for you. But only as long as it's nothing too strong. He's ordering everything, actually. Good friends with the barkeeper."

Lacuna looked at Sonai, wide-eyed at the implication.

Sonai rolls her eyes at Lacuna's expression as she says, "Soda." As per usual.

Lacuna calms down a little from Sonai's request. She turns back to Ala. "And I would like to order a glass of apple juice, if possible."

"Gotcha! See you guys in a second!" Ala ran back towards the concession station.

Watching her leave, Lacuna asked, "Is the lack of other faeries the reason that you don't like parties?"

"No, I just said that there are usually fae in places like this. I don't like parties 'cause I don't wanna be in the middle of large human gatherings."

"I see…"

"Anyways," Sonai chided. "Who over the age of ten orders apple juice? Do you even like apple juice?"

"Yes, why else would I order it then?"

Soon enough, Ala was back, rushing over and exclaiming, "Here's your drinks." She set a ginger ale can and a glass of apple juice on the table. "Bye!" She ran again, nearly bumping into someone searching for a bowling ball rack.

Sonai observed the sight before turning back to Lacuna. "I don't know. But you were so weirded out by the mention of alcohol, only to get a drink that's whiskey colored." She smirked. "Maybe it was subconscious?"

Normally, Lacuna would feel scandalized at the assumption. Instead, she smiled back. It started out as a small, close mouthed smile. Then a sliver of white appeared, normally unwilling to show itself even in her happiest moments. "Now this is the Sonai I know. Welcome back."

Sonai blinked in surprise. "I, uh… didn't know you could do that…"

"Hmm?"

"It's so weird to see you smile."

"Ok, then I will stop."

"No!" she yelled. "I mean, there's nothing bad about it, it's just that you don't usually do it, so it's just kinda… weird to see?"

"You are behaving strangely again."

Sonai sighed. "Only because you are."

Lacuna shrugged. "In relation to the previous topic, I was convinced you would've ordered an alcoholic beverage."

"I know I'm not usually one to follow rules, but you should really stop assuming things about me. Plus, that stuff messes with Veil Sight." She then looks in the direction of the party room, with a far off look, perhaps reminiscent of whatever wild event allowed to understand this fact.

Eventually, Ala returned to the group of booths for good, bringing Delilah with her. The two girls then challenged Delilah's boyfriend, Jason, to a bowling competition. A couple other people joined in. Although Lacuna and Sonai were both invited, they declined.

"I just want to watch," Lacuna replied.

As she sips at her apple juice, Sonai unconsciously stares. Underneath the kaleidoscope-esque lights of the bowling alley, Lacuna's features stood starkly in comparison to all the other humans, her coily hair and mahogany skin glistening. Sonai began to notice aspects of her that she didn't really pay attention to before. She knew that as an Arius, the girl had most likely been physically trained. The sleeveless turtleneck she wore revealed the entirety of her arms, one crossed along the table, the other raised as she drank. And the longer Sonai stared, the more she began to notice the visible thickness of said arms. It was something she originally thought was a figment of her imagination, flickers of density coming and going with the sheer quickness of Lacuna's movements and baggy clothing. However, in this docile moment, Sonai began to realize that the woman sitting across from her was—quite muscular. Absolutely shredded. While Sonai herself possessed some faint musculature, attributed to both her many escapades between the realms and a hint of Glamour, her arms were nowhere near as pronounced as Lacuna's.

A sudden inclination of thirst came over her, persuading Sonai to snatch up her soda. The drink did little to combat it.

The party had been ongoing for around an hour now and Ala's bowling match came to a close. Unfortunately for her, it was Delilah who won, just like she did during their air hockey match several minutes before. Ala attempted to avoid having both embarrassing defeats be known to Lacuna, Sonai, and the rest of their corner, but the discordance of friendly gloating let them know anyway. The pizza arrived, the boxes currently in the party room, yet five and a half slices were suddenly on Lacuna's plate. She consumed them with an unnecessary haste. Sonai handed her a napkin with a small chuckle.

The event was going well for all the humans commuting in the building, yet a glaring issue was present. There were two significant individuals who had yet to arrive.

Ala, who was previously laughing with another friend of Delilah's, looked towards the entrance way. She briefly excused herself from the conversation to announce, "They're finally here!" to the entire group. A moment later, the two people that Lacuna and Sonai had come for were directly in front of them. They all gave false waves of friendliness to one another, waiting until Ala left again. Hopefully another bowling match was going to start soon.

"It's pretty bold of you to come out of hiding," Sonai chimed, watching Ala gather more bowlers out of the corner of her eye.

Jaw clenched, Tobi replied, "We didn't expect you to think I'd be here. Party's aren't my thing."

"What are you doing here?" Kelisha demanded, standing as a shield between the two fae. Tobi cautiously put a hand on her shoulder.

"I'm not gonna hurt you, not here. We just wanna talk."

Lacuna nodded in agreement.

Sonai shuffled back to Lacuna's side of the booth, letting Kelisha and Tobi slide into her old space. The girls were huddled like two separate teams in a relay race.

But for one pair, the act of losing here could mean death.

Tobi seethed. "I already told you, I'm not going back to Melterra."

"And I already told you, you don't have a choice. If you were any other fae, I wouldn't care that you wanna run into the arms of a human. You could fraternize with witches all you want." A hint of disgust entered her voice. "But the day you decided to enter the Roots of the Great Tree, you sealed your fate. Your existence in the universe is finished, one way or another."

Both Lacuna and Kelisha looked between the two fae in shock. The latter gasped, "I didn't realize it was that serious…"

Scoffing, Sonai sneered, "Then why would you even take Tobi as your familiar in the first place? You just didn't care what she'd been through, just saw a fae in desperation and took advantage, huh?" She laughs, twisted and insinuating. "Typical…"

"Excuse me?" Kelisha's face twists disgustedly at the accusation. "You don't know a thing about me and Tobi's friendship!"

"Maybe, but it doesn't look like you know much either."

And here it was. The teasing, smart-mouthed persona that evoked smirking towards those who opposed her with inciting rudeness. Sonai looked a lot more like herself now, her previous nervous slump fading as the conversation continued. At first, Lacuna simply thought she wanted Sonai to act normally because it was unusual to see her shy. But now? Now, she began to realize that she simply preferred her current personality. Meek shyness and shivering didn't look right spinning in the fiery eyes of someone as bold as Sonai.

On the other hand, she knew that Kelisha didn't deserve to receive the force of Sonai's reawakening. While she was entirely unsure of what to think in regards to Tobi, Lacuna's opinion of Kelisha was neutral. She was kind and helpful, protective of a fae who was in extreme danger. But that was exactly the problem. Although Lacuna had begun to doubt many of the teachings in Revenali, the negative opinions of witches had embedded themselves deep within her mind. And this concept was further amplified by Sonai's reaction to Kelisha. Her opinion as a faerie was entirely negative as well, insinuating the familiars were taken advantage of by witches. No matter which version of witches as a concept she analyzed, the same conclusion appeared.

"But aren't you familiar too?" Tobi asked genuinely.

"Wow! Don't you ever imply something like that again!" Sonai growled. "I would never allow myself to be a slave to a human."

She gestures to Lacuna. "Why are you working with her then? She's a human, right?"

"The current situation has pushed us to follow one another. This arrangement simply relates to a common goal," Lacuna replied.

Sonai nodded. "She just wants the information you stole. And even though I kinda wanna hear too, I'm just here to catch you. Plus, Lacuna isn't really human."

Tobi observes Lacuna with a hum. "I was starting to think that. I noticed how her aura is a little off-putting compared to other humans, but I thought it was just because you were nearby."

"I guess the aura of the Olan would be off-putting, huh?"

"What?" Tobi exclaimed. "That's impossible!"

"We're not so sure it is actually."

Tobi stared at Lacuna for a long time. Time stood still within her blue eyes, contemplating the validity of Sonai's statement. She could see her as a faerie, maybe even a half-faerie. But not the Olan. There was no way, not in this era. Right?

"I see…" Tobi pondered. "But I won't tell you what I know, unless you allow me to be free."

"Of course… not." Sonai rolled her eyes. "It's Lacuna who wants the information, not me. Like I said, I'm just here to get you. But you are the only faerie other than the queen who knows what the Olan is. That being said, even if I were to learn what it meant, I'm sure the queen would trust me. In fact, I could probably ask her myself later." She leaned back, emphasizing her attitude. "But all in all, it doesn't matter much to me because I have a job to do."

Tobi's jaw clenched again, and Kelisha put her hand on her shoulder. Tobi turned to look at her, blue eyes looking at brown eyes, silently asking, *"How are we going to get out of this?"*

"But…" Sonai smirked, turning into a devious smile. "I've always been a fae of the Unseelie Court at heart, even though they're combined now."

The concept of an Unseelie Court and Seelie Court existing in the fae realm was known in Revenali. Jordan had explained it to her nearly a month ago. Rude and violet fae were Unseelie, while kind, unsuspecting fae were Seelie. Both were considered dangerous; both were eliminated just the same. However, the idea of these courts combining was bewildering to Lacuna. What did it mean for the monarchy?

"The queen simply told me to get rid of you for the knowledge you possess. Her exact words. If you tell me what you know, I'll be able to give you freedom through the act of being remade."

Tobi gulped, looking at her wide-eyed.

Kelisha and Lacuna were once again confused. Lacuna stammered, "Are you—how— what does being remade pertain to?" She was almost as bewildered as Tobi.

"Basically, a faerie's form is rewinded to when they were first created. They forget all of their memories. Personalities are usually the same, but that's also based on how they're raised. In Melterra, most things repeat themselves. So if Tobi were to go back, which she can't by the way, then she would be completely the same. But in the human realm, she could change drastically. It's a gamble overall."

Kelisha looks at her with an expression in a mix between sadness and disgust. "How does a person understand they've lived before if they have no memories? That's like the same thing as dying then reincarnating. How is this different from her being executed?"

"It's extremely different," Lacuna replied. "Execution for fae describes being erased from existence. Most fae either live forever, or go through thousands of semi-reincarnations. The only way to truly get rid of a fae is to destroy their existence in general. Unlike humans, who may possibly have an afterlife, fae do not." She looks at Sonai. "But I had no idea fae could be remade."

"So Tobi's only choices were to either forget everything, or stop existing."

"Yep. And if she chooses to do so, she will not be allowed back into Melterra."

"Then where will I go in the human realm?"

Sonai points to Kelisha. "Back with your disgusting human. I can curse you so that even after the recreation ritual, your souls will be connected. A fitting fate."

Tobi exhales, eyes shining with happiness. Happiness that Kelisha can't comprehend.

"So she will really forget all of her memories? How does…" her voice trails off.

"Yep! And her form will revert that of when she was first created. Nearly powerless. You could do whatever you wanted."

"Stop speaking to her like that! She's not some sort of abusive monster like an Arius!"

Lacuna turned towards her, feeling slightly offended.

"But… I…" Stuttering as she spoke, all her emotions mingling together. She took a deep breath and collected herself. Soon after, she confidently declared, "I accept your idea. I'll give you the knowledge you seek on the condition that I'm remade entirely as a familiar for Kelisha."

CHAPTER 10

The day Kelisha met Tobi was the day she truly grew as a witch.

A few years ago, Kelisha had been traveling, searching for an enchanted forest. One which was overflowing with faerie energy, and its forest floor hopefully blanketed by the soft glow of unusual lilies. A forest that sat directly on the Veil. She was in search of ingredients for an elixir she planned to cook up soon. Kelisha trudged through nearly every forest in Podim, Ohio. And all the effort was for a simple magic-infused healing salve. Although it wasn't going to be used on anyone anytime soon, it was an essential spell for any traveling magic user to know.

So as Kelisha marched on through more ordinary woods, she stayed vigilant for the sight of glowing flowers or strange structures. Her jeans were scratched by thorny bushes; the cuffs at the bottom patched with dried mud. They were now barely holding up at keeping her tired legs protected from the outside elements. But at least that was what they were made for. The main problem within her choice of outfit wasn't the bottom, but rather, the entire top half. She shouldn't have worn a flowy white blouse that day.

Kelisha completely understood looking for ingredients meant hiking through muddy woods, but she couldn't help herself. The *modern witch* outfit idea she saw online a few days ago was just too stylish for her to pass up wearing on one adventure. And the fae liked stylish, right? She hoped a nice outfit would persuade them to be kinder to her.

"It looked so cute in the mirror this morning," Kelisha thought to herself as another white thread got caught on tree bark. She sighed, "At least it was cheap..."

Yet even cheaper was the crown jewel of her outfit. To truly match the *modern witch* aesthetic, atop her braided hair loosely sat a cartoon witch hat made of violet felt fabric. A gold buckle, made from ribbon, wrapped around the hat unevenly. She bought it from the dollar store, and since it was from the kids section, it didn't really fit. Even now, it threatened to leap off her head like it was sentient.

Despite her many attempts at improving her status as a witch, Kelisha began to feel like she was working towards becoming a clown instead. The longer she walked through the forest, the more her main goal behind finding the flowers morphed into simply making sure her previous hikes weren't in vain. And now, she just wanted to rush home and change.

Suddenly, she spotted a soft glow reflecting off of a tree trunk. Kelisha dashed over, nearly slipping on mud before realizing that what she saw wasn't a lily.

A glowing, feminine figure slumped against the dark bark of the tree. She appeared semi-transparent, blue skin slowly fading with each heaving breath she took. Hair covered her face, flowing in a blue to purple ombre. It was crystalline in nature, like a waterfall. Large, finned ears protruded from behind the waterfall. Looking at the appearance of the evidently fae being, she appeared to be a water nymph.

Kelisha spoke up, low, attempting to not startle the faerie. "Um… hello? Are you hurt?"

The fae struggled, holding up her head slowly. She coughed out, "How can you see me?"

Kelisha kept her voice leveled, speaking slowly so that she wouldn't stutter. "I'm a witch. I presume that you are one of the fae folk?"

"Yes." Her response was simple. "Do you have ill intentions?"

"I have no ill intentions."

"Then tell me, what is your name?" She held her head up fully. Her blue eyes narrowed, attempting to look directly into Kelisha's.

Kelisha averts her gaze as she replies. "I can not tell you my name. Upon your tongue, I choose to remain nameless."

The fae growls, lowly, perhaps not meaning to give away her trick through a show of frustration. Kelisha knew fae could feed on the energy of humans, slurping their life essence away directly through the windows to their souls. It had become obvious to her that the faerie sitting in front of her intended to use her magical energy as fuel, yet failed miserably.

"Why did you just try to hurt me?" Kelisha tried to hold in her laughter, not wanting to offend the faerie in case she had more devastating powers hidden away. But her attempt also failed, just like the faerie in front of her. A short giggle escaped her, the sound echoing through the forest.

"Don't you dare…" The faerie wraps her arms around herself, letting out a deep, shuddering breath, "…laugh at me human." The attempt at appearing intimidating was also pathetic.

Guilt crawled through Kelisha's poor outfit choice towards the tip of her hat. The fae in front of her was obviously suffering immensely, desperate to keep herself from phasing through the Veil. And she had the audacity to laugh. If this was her attempt at befriending fae, then all she would end up with was enemies.

"I'm sorry. I didn't mean to laugh." It was partially true. Kelisha really was sorry, at least within her own mind. Would half-truths be taboo for the fae too?

The faerie took another deep breath. "Well, what are you doing here in the forest?"

"I'm searching for flowers. I need citrine lilies for healing salves."

"I see." She looked down, hair falling in front of her face again as she murmured. "It must be nice to walk around this beautiful forest without worry or pain."

"Yes, it is nice."

The two remained silent for a moment. The faerie suddenly lets out a sharp wince, her flickering form becoming more sporadic.

"Do you need help?"

"I don—" She winces again, fading completely for a second. Upon reappearing, her waterfall of hair no longer conceals her face. Blue eyes gaze anxiously at Kelisha. "I think we should make a deal."

Kelisha looks at her indirectly with suspicion. "What are you asking of me for this deal?"

"If you allow me to feed on a fraction of your energy, I'll allow you to summon me whenever you desire. I could be an assistant for you."

She perks up. "Like a familiar?"

"Yes, essentially." One of her slender fingers tapped quickly against her arm.

Kelisha thought about it for a little bit, looking down at the tapping hand. "Hmm… the deal you make sounds promising, but I'm not sure if I should accept the offer." Something about the deal was off to her.

"Ah, I see. Certainly a mage such as yourself has dozens of fae following you around, begging to become your familiar?"

Kelisha laughs, this time loud and clear. "Oh! No. Definitely not! I've.. um…never had a familiar before. It's why I'm unsure about your offer. And I'm not sure if I should trust you…" She holds her hands up defensively upon realizing the connotations of her statement. "But I'm not trying to say that you're up to no good or anything like that! It's just that I'm not familiar with the fae folk."

"Don't lie to me," the demand muttered, intended to not sound as threatening. "If you believe I'm suspicious, just tell me."

"I'm—" She quickly stops herself from apologizing, shaking away the statement. "How can I be sure your deal isn't a trap?"

Another wince was torn out of her, the desperation that sat behind their eyes increased tenfold. It began to show itself in the form of tears. "I promise upon my soul that as a faerie of the Seelie Court, the deal that I wish to make with you includes everything I've told you so far. So will you accept it or not?"

Fae can't break promises.

"Ok. As long as the fraction of energy you take from me is small, then I will agree to your offer."

The faerie shook her head happily. "Yes. Now then, hold out your hand. The one with the bracelet on it."

Hesitantly, Kelisha lifted her arm, allowing the faerie to take a good look at her bracelet. It was one that had been gifted to her from her great grandmother, during her sixteenth birthday. She passed away shortly after that.

After analyzing the bracelet, the faerie said, "This shall become my settling instrument. Wherever you need me, simply use the bracelet." She gently placed her hands on it, her remaining magic energy flowing through it and tickling Kelisha's arm. The silver color of the bracelet began to morph into a dim lilac. Soon after, she began to fade again. "For the next month, you may refer to me as Tobi."

Month? Oh, so that was the offness she felt. What she forgot to ask about. The time frame.

Kelisha sighed, bested by the weakened fae. "Is there anything else you need from me, Tobi?"

The faerie was nearly completely transparent at this point. "For now, there's nothing." She smiled. "See you soon." Her entire form dissipated, transforming into small glittering specks. They flew over and attached themselves to the bracelet like dew on a leaf. Upon doing so, the lilac color became lavender, signifying Tobi's entrance into the bracelet. Kelisha looked at the color for a long time.

And for a long time, she wouldn't see Tobi again either. Or the flowers she came to look for in the first place.

No matter how hard she strove to find them, there were no citrine lilies in her immediate area of the human realm. She spent hours searching far and wide for an area in the woods with glowing flowers. Eventually, she left, but she came back the next day wondering if their appearance was time related. After a while, she moved on, searching in more forests before deciding that her current skill level wouldn't allow her to sense a section of the forest intertwined with the Veil. Throughout her entire extended journey, Kelisha made many attempts at calling Tobi from within the bracelet. There were the original, kind attempts, with many *please*s and *I'm sorry to bother you*'s. For a moment, she thought these attempts were worth a shot. Maybe there was a secret rule amongst the fae which would allow them to accept her kindness. This was a rather ill-considered thought; Kelisha already understood such words wouldn't work.

The concept behind human formalities was not something that the average fae enjoyed. In fact, it was well known within magic communities that *manners* were something that fae culture actively contested. From what Kelisha had heard from other witches, the concept of manners is denounced on the other side of the Veil because it's often disingenuous. *Please* doesn't automatically mean someone is kind and *thank you* doesn't actually mean they're actually thankful. For beings who often spent their eternal days fighting over resources like wolves, striving to engage in endless pleasures, letting their emotions—or lack thereof—run as wild as themselves, such formalities were entirely unnecessary.

Human children learned the etiquette of politeness and manners from birth. Playing with other children, learning to share and respect their parents. Most fae didn't have parents to respect. Sharing was rare. And they lived in a society where respect was stolen, not earned. Manners were simply social customs, rather than needs of life. Except for those who wanted to pretend, of course.

And when one fae wants something, all others must be wary and respect it, for that is when the needs of their lives appear. It's how their many rules came to be. How their elaborate hexes and their curses fell upon the realms of the earth.

All fae had a want, a desire to have one thing they considered more beautiful and important than anything else in the entire world. A treasure. And when they found that thing, they would cherish it forever and fight to the death to protect it. Like the dragons of fairy tales—who were in fact, fellow fae—they would hoard their precious thing tightly, even in the cases where the thing wasn't actually an inanimate object at all.

Humans could become the special thing of a faerie. And much of what the magic community talked about involved the stalkings, kidnappings, and sometimes killings done by fae who wanted a human all for themselves.

Animalistic in nature, although many were humanoid in appearance, they lived how they wanted to and usually died how they wanted to as well—if they died at all. Both benevolent and malevolent all at same time, their passions wrapped within the ancient spiritual threads of the Veil. Fae were not to be messed with by those unfamiliar with their ways.

Kelisha currently found herself in an odd contract with an odd faerie, who had yet to reveal herself again.

While the situation made her feel wary, Kelisha didn't entirely feel scared by it. She'd often end up using Tobi's existence within her bracelet to ground herself. Before Tobi arrived, Kelisha would often talk to herself as a means of calming her nerves. She felt that false companionship was necessary as she traveled around, searching for ingredients in areas that might have more dangerous fae. *"How does this look?"* she'd say, thrusting her bracelet at strange trees, hoping that the being inside would finally answer her requests. If Kelisha were truly honest with herself, she'd have to admit that her speech and actions revealed her life as somewhat pitiful. Few friends, few hobbies outside of magic and poor outfit choices. All to focus on attaining full-fledged witch-hood, as backwards as it might sound.

Luckily for Kelisha, the day of Tobi's reappearance eventually came. Unluckily for her, it was in a way that involved a situation she had desperately been trying to avoid.

During what would've originally been an ordinary forest hike, Kelisha found herself by a pond. Expansive, it sat in a clearing, strangely swallowed up by fog. The sight was quite unusual, since there hadn't been a call for foggy weather that day. And perhaps even stranger than the fog were the various geese that sat on its surface.

They made no noise. They didn't flap their wings or nuzzle against one another. Their faint treading along the water's surface refused to create splashes. Their eyes appeared empty from Kelisha's spot on the pond's shore. Eyes Kelisha felt afraid to look directly into.

Almost as if they were fae.

But they weren't. And it was Tobi who let her know why.

Out of the corner of her eye, Kelisha saw Tobi at last, her glowing aquatic features stark against the fog. "We need to leave." She stated plainly, and quite suddenly. "This is the territory of someone dangerous, I can feel it."

Kelisha wanted to yell and demand Tobi for answers regarding her nearly two week long disappearance. But when she turned to look at her, she saw another figure. Floating over the pond was a shadow. A deep, dark shadow, vaguely humanoid and wavy, staring at her from across the water. Its eyes were just as deep as their figure, and appeared as a similar blue to Tobi's own. The only difference was the malevolent aura emitted by its glare, implicating carnivorous desires. Upon touching down on the water, all of the geese *sank* instantaneously in a slow bubbling motion.

"Oh. My. G—" Kelisha couldn't get her words out before the unknown creature *sprinted* at her. It was upon her within the span of a second from across ten meters of water. Its shadowy claws mere inches away from Kelisha's face.

Had Tobi not been there with her, Kelisha would surely have lost her life that day.

With her magic, Tobi encased the creature in some of its own stagnant pond water. Tobi seemed to struggle, and whether or not it was due to the strength of the being or the weight of the water was unknown to Kelisha. Either way, the capsule Tobi made wouldn't hold off the creature for much longer. The sheer power of a simple sprint was unbelievable, unlike anything Kelisha had ever heard of before. Or at least what she had heard of for normal fae. It was possible that the creature here may have been some sort of guardian. A powerful sort of fae with strength rumored to be similar to that of demi-gods or the Faerie Queen. Legends about guardians circulated around rapidly in witch communities, perhaps fortifying their powers like a curse.

But if this creature was in fact a guardian, then what was it guarding?

For now, Kelisha wouldn't get to know. The creature began to break through Tobi's capsule. Kelisha screamed, "Tobi!" urging the faerie to run as well.

"You need to leave!"

"It's gonna kill you if I do!" She took out the wand attached to her hip. "I'll help you!"

Gurgling sounds resounded from the creature's throat. Tobi made a terrified face, replying "The human is not a threat to you." So the gurgling sounds were language, one that Kelisha couldn't seem to understand.

"Human, I need you to get away from here immediately! It's mainly because you're here that they're angered. So jus—" The creature had gotten free, suddenly taking hold of Tobi's neck.

"Tobi!" Kelisha yelled as she rushed towards the creature, with an energy blast forming on her staff. Before turning their attention to Kelisha, the creature reached a hand towards the center of Tobi's chest. She squirmed within its grasp, fighting desperately to prevent something that Kelisha hadn't once known was possible. Suddenly, the creature reached its hand *through* Tobi's chest, nearly pulling out a bright light. As the movement happened, Tobi began to fizzle quickly, becoming glittery like she did when she first entered Kelisha's bracelet. Kelisha couldn't comprehend what was being taken from Tobi, but she knew it meant bad news.

"NO!" Kelisha launched the magic at the creature, praying that it would make it in time. The creature turned its head towards her, in a similar way that the dead geese had. It became hyper focused on the screeching of Kelisha's human voice. Disgusted by it.

Before dropping Tobi to rush at Kelisha, the creature snagged a piece of the light in Tobi's chest, then headed straight for the magic blast. Tobi fell with a short cry.

Kelisha once again just barely dodged the creature's attack. Was there any way to defeat it? Or at least, trap it and have enough time to run away? At first Kelisha believed that if she and Tobi teamed up, then beating it in battle would be possible. Now, Tobi might not be strong enough to fight back.

However, Kelisha failed to realize the exact strength that an individual faerie could possess. In one final effort, Tobi put up another capsule of water around the creature. She struggled up onto her feet and screamed, wordlessly. Kelisha ran over to her, allowing her now fractured essence to reenter the bracelet. She dashed towards the edge of the forest, away from fog, stagnant ponds, dead geese, and the gurgling sound of a shadowy guardian, who's presence felt as though it had been directly behind her during her last couple seconds of running.

Once she finally thought like the coast was clear, Kelisha slumped against the brick walls of a nearby building. This entire area was one of the many metroparks in Podim, Ohio. She tiredly looked down at the bracelet, and asked, "Tobi? Are you ok?"

"I'm not sure." Tobi's voice could be heard from directly inside Kelisha's mind.

"Why didn't you use this telepathy before? Couldn't you hear me talking before?" Kelisha felt too tired to yell at Tobi for ignoring her previously.

"Energy conservation, human."

She hummed. "I don't want to be known as just 'human' anymore, Tobi. I want you to call me Kelisha from now on."

Tobi was silent for a second. "Ok then, Kelisha. For saving my life, I want to offer you something."

"You also saved my life, so you don't have to offer anything. We're pretty much even."

"No." Tobi's voice was beholden. "I nearly died there. Saving me from that experience is more helpful than what I did."

Kelisha thought about it for a moment. "Well then, I do have one request."

"Yes?"

Kelisha smiled tiredly, taking a deep breath. "I want you to be my familiar for real, Tobi. Not just an assistant for a month." But wordlessly she was truly saying: *I'd like you to be my friend, Tobi.*

From within the bracelet, soul echoing directly into Kelisha's mind, Tobi replied: "I would like that too, Kelisha."

CHAPTER 11

What was death like for creatures who could never truly die—whose souls were trapped in an endless cycle?

What could end that cycle of rebirth?

What does the act of remaking a creature consist of?

What would happen to their body?

Their mind?

Their soul?

T The day after Deliliah's party, the four girls found themselves huddled up in Podim University's library, debating on the concept of existence itself. Through all the questioning and muted quarreling behind the tall walls of books, one could conclude that existence was a major topic for fae and magic users alike. Yet the topic of recreation was an entirely different realm of thought. It was a territory partially unmarked, even by the fae who naturally possessed the ability to perform the action themselves. Often due to the way it affected their memories. Thus, over the course of their conversation, the group concluded that the most important concept behind recreation was its direct relation to memories.

When an event happens, but there was no one around to see it, then did it happen at all?

Kelisha knew that Tobi would forget her, but would she forget Tobi too? It was a genuine possibility after all. There were fae within the universe who could erase the existence of others and themselves from the minds of humans with the simplest of magics. But luckily for the worried girl, Sonai confirmed that this wouldn't be the case.

"So about your last question…" Sonai flipped through a strange-looking book she found. "It's usually executed fae who have their existence erased, but it also depends on how the execution happens."

"How so?" asked Kelisha, as Sonai finally stopped her flipping.

"We can talk about that later. For now, we're gonna need to get three items for Tobi's recreation." Sonai placed the book flat on the table for everyone else to see, gesturing to the two pages. Inside was a diagram of an unusual winged creature; Lacuna guessed that it was meant to be a depiction of a faerie. The figure stood in the anatomical position, with many arrows branching off of its body towards short, informative text boxes.

"What does it mean?" Lacuna asked, despite being in the process of actively reading over the textboxes herself. The diagram detailed body parts, sections where the author decided magic should be located, and other things of that nature.

"I was just about to tell y'all, so give me a second! First, this book is super inaccurate. Don't ever believe what any one of these…" She picked up the book again to take a quick look at the title, "…*Legends of the Fae Folk for Beginner Witches*, type of books have to say about fae like me and Tobi. But, I will say there are a few things in this picture right here," the book was dropped back on the table with an audible thud, "that are gonna be important for you." Sonai pointed a judgemental finger at Kelisha. "And so like I said a second ago, we're gonna need three things for Tobi."

As Sonai pointed to the top of the diagram, Lacuna said, "The mind." She circled around the diagram and Lacuna said, "The body." And finally, Sonai pointed directly at the heart as Lacuna said, "The soul." Just like they were labeled.

"And what about them?" Tobi asked.

"We're gonna need a source to mold your body, convert your mind, and preserve your soul."

Lacuna looked down at the diagram again. She analyzed the contours of the creature's body, the way in which blue and purple veins trailed throughout it, and how its hair waved around various limbs in ringlets. Even with her limited knowledge, Lacuna could also understand how inaccurate the diagram was for whatever faerie it was meant to depict. Yet something about the book and its eccentric diagrams reminded her of the Oracle and their office. How their questions were often nonsensical like the crooked wings of the illustrated creature, and how their concept of souls and existence could be even more complex than anything the four girls had thought about today.

"…So the idea revolves around emotions, Lacuna," stated the Oracle one summer evening six years ago. "People claim to feel emotions within their hearts, despite science stating that they stem from the brain. It's why theologists and magic practitioners have come up with the concept of souls." They were holding a small plastic orb. As they kneaded it with their hands, it began to glow brightly. "Some believe that this is what the physical manifestation of a soul looks like."

"Why is it glowing?" asked young Lacuna.

"It's glowing because it's magical. Plain and simple."

"But isn't an object having magic properties just to do so too simple for faeries? At least, that is what you told me before."

"Hmm… perhaps you could say that. But human souls and fae souls are different."

Lacuna tilted her head, folding the long sleeves of her temple robe onto her lap, legs crossed in her position on the floor.

The Oracle let out a small chuckle. "Both human and fae souls determine magical ability. The brighter it glows, the more magic it has. But only humans have an afterlife for their souls to go to. In a way, faeries are already in their afterlife. Some humans can even turn into fae once they die."

"Really?"

"Yes, you can find recounts of incidents like that in the library."

Lacuna scanned the desk area directly behind them. "Do you have any books about it here in the office?"

"The important books I keep here aren't meant for children, they're much too advanced so you mustn't search in here." The Oracle's voice had a hint of a threatening nature, not aggressive, simply parental.

Lacuna folded her sleeves over one another again, fidgeting.

"Now, the souls of humans differ greatly from fae in other ways too. Human souls constantly search for new spiritual heights." They lowered the orb towards Lacuna. "Often, it seems like certain humans want to become so powerful, they can become gods."

"Is it possible?"

They shook their head. "Certainly not. It's completely incomprehensible. Luckily for Revenali, fae don't think this way. And there's no need for them to. Despite their strong magical bodies, the additional properties in the souls of fae are weak. On the contrary, while the bodies of humans are weak, their souls are strong. And the minds of both beings can be changed and molded in any way they see fit." Behind their mask, Lacuna could almost see a glinting, mischievous smile.

As she looked up, the Oracle's hand fell upon her head, smoothing over her curls. The action reminded her of Reno and his mother for a moment. But she refrained from leaning into the touch. The Oracle wasn't like Reno's mother. They could never be.

"It makes one wonder, what the result of a fae soul and human soul combining in perfect union would result in."

Lacuna blinked up at them. "But... I thought there were already examples of fae and humans having children together?"

"Yes, that's true." The Oracle retracted their hand. "But their souls can't be considered perfect in any capacity." They suddenly stood from their chair, making their way towards one of their large windows overlooking the ocean. Lacuna stood up too and followed. "Most fae-human combinations created previously would often result in full fae with notably human-like appearances, such as Changelings, or humans with additional magic prowess. Yet such humans would have even weaker bodies, often dying a few years after birth." They shook their head despondently. "This happens because neither soul was strong enough. What's needed is the soul of an exceptionally strong faerie and a strong-willed soul of a human." Their masked face looked down at her, through her, as if looking directly into her soul. "We need a combination of the strongest of said souls. One that will result in a truly perfect half-fae."

It should've been during this moment that Lacuna realized the truth of her existence. Yet what reason did she have to question it at the time? The Oracle had given her their full attention; the lesson of that day much more dynamic than anything previously discussed. It was one of the few times in her life that they actually physically interacted with her, allowing their gloved fingers to float along her head of hair in what should've been an endearing parental moment.

Within the Podim library, miles away from the temple, Lacuna wondered if the Oracle had ever held her as a baby. Even despite claiming it was mainly the temple maids who took care of her, they would've had to at some point, right? She tried to imagine the untight, calculative, and unempathetic Oracle holding a baby, watching her play with genuine affection. Only to then curse her future self with the burden of needing to kill those just like her. Alongside thinking about this ironic predicament, Lacuna was also forced to recall how neglectful her childhood had truly been. Filled with featherlike touches from gloved hands and a masked face pretending to be immersed in literature.

She could help but doubt more positive beliefs about the Oracle immensely now.

In contrast with these thoughts, Lacuna knew that the Olan wasn't simply a half-fae. So what did the combination of a strong fae soul and human soul truly mean?

"I'm pretty sure using all three of our powers at once will be enough to remake Tobi's mind and body," Sonai stated as she gestured around the table. "But preserving her soul will be way harder. We're gonna need something, or someone, that represents Tobi's existence."

Kelisha looked at Sonai, dumbfounded. "I'm sorry, I'm going to need an example of that, because…what? How can an item represent someone's existence?"

"It can also be a person who represents their existence," Lacuna reminded her.

"What she means is," stated Tobi, "the item must be something that shows I've made a mark on the world. Like a treasure or project."

"But not everyone has done something like that."

"Yes they have," corrected Sonai.

"How so?"

"All beings have something that shows they've existed in the universe. It can be something small and it can be something large, but it must be something of extreme importance to the being." She brought her chair closer. "For example, let's say you had a teddy bear. If the bear had a lot of history in your family and you kept it for years on end, it's possible that the bear could be a mark of your existence. This is what Tobi was talking about when she mentioned treasure. A mark of existence can also be a physical representation of something metaphorical, like… I don't know… ballet?" She thought about it for a moment. "Yeah. So, if you really liked dancing, then ballet shoes could be a mark of your existence, even if it's not the shoes themselves that were important to you. Just ballet dancing."

"Ok, I think I get it now, but how would we know what item represents Tobi?" Kelisha then turned to Tobi. "Unless you already have an idea, of course."

Tobi shook her head.

"It's this final part that makes the recreation process so difficult. Even though all beings have a mark of existence, most never truly know what it is. And there isn't an exact way of knowing either. You just gotta guess." Sonai leaned back. "So before we start searching, do you guys have any more questions or concerns?"

Tobi shifted uncomfortably in her chair. "Yeah, I have one."

Sonai gave her a tentative look.

"How intact does my soul have to be for the ritual."

"Huh?" Sonai sat up straight again. "All the way intac—what are you talking about? Who does a ritual like this on someone without a complete soul?"

Tobi nervously chuckled. "Uh, then we have a problem…"

"Great," she said sarcastically. "Lemme hear it."

Tobi proceeded to explain the guardian incident from a few years ago. The battle, the area and most importantly, the part where Tobi got her soul snatched.

"Since then, I haven't been able to access my nymph form."

"So that's why I haven't seen you like that since that day?" Kesliha exclaimed. "Why didn't you tell me?"

"I didn't want you to worry or go back to the pond. You know they would've killed you."

Kelisha wanted to argue, but decided against it with a sigh. She put her hand on Tobi's shoulder and looked at her wordlessly. Tobi glanced at her before turning her attention back to the rest of the group.

"You know, you're extremely lucky your entire soul wasn't shattered," Sonai stated.

Tobi looked away from Kelisha and nodded. So did Lacuna.

As an Arius, Lacuna understood what the concept of shattered souls represented. While many fae could come back to life after death, it was their soul that kept them tethered to the earth, preventing them from fading out of existence. Most considered the same to be true for humans. Yet while humans with shattered souls would often be missing something, like certain emotions or talents, fae with shattered souls would begin to morph. Slowly but surely, they'd turn into more dangerous versions of themselves, previous malevolence increasing tenfold, magical prowess nearly incomprehensible. Had Tobi's soul been harmed anymore, she may have been this way too.

It was the elimination of souls that was mainly responsible for the elimination of fae. If the soul wasn't completely destroyed, then all of the previously mentioned issues could occur. It's something that Lacuna felt the most nervous about before officially becoming an Arius. During her lessons, she was recommended to imagine a small pixie transforming into a gargantuan beast, warped and abhorrent, if stabbed in the chest but not finished off quickly.

"If we want this to work, we're gonna have to go and get that fragment of Tobi's soul back. Lacuna and I will go, since we're stronger." Sonai looked at Lacuna with a smirk. "Do you think you can take on a forest guardian?"

In her usual passive tone, yet with a hint of challenge, Lacuna replied ironically, "It's what I was raised for."

"I guess I'll actually get to see how you fight then." She propped her chin upon her hand from where it now leaned against the table. "No more getting distracted by the word Olan, ok?"

Lacuna gave her a sharp nod, flashing a small smile. "Yes ma'am."

Both girls looked each other in the eye, gaze holding one another there as whispers of their involuntary obligations whisked themselves past story books and into their current goals.

Technically, the two of them were still not friends. Lacuna continued to question whether or not she would return to Revenali after gaining the information she needed. Would understanding the truth of her existence truly be enough to make her abandon all she's ever known?

Tobi and Kelisha looked between the two in disbelief, before looking at one another in silent understanding.

Sonai and Lacuna, noticing their strange reaction, broke eye contact in surprise. "What is it?" Sonai asked as Lacuna looked at the two on the opposite side of the table.

"It's nothing," Tobi and Kelisha said in unison.

They were obviously lying, but there was no need to question it further. At the moment, more important business needed to be taken care of.

Sonai helped Kelisha determine the exact location of the nature center she visited during the time of the incident. In the main area was a small, quaint, brick building. It sat in the middle of a clearing surrounded by colorful flowers. Various benches were placed through the park area for the park rangers and visitors alike.

"It was this area that made me think I could find the healing citrine lilies nearby," Kelisha exclaimed as she pointed to the picture on her phone, zooming into the flowers.

As the group did more research on the area, a surprising result came up. Supposedly, there wasn't a pond located in the area. Just birch trees, bushes and flowers.

"It's because the Veil is creating a barrier between our differing eyes, human eyes and fae eyes. We'll notice it once we get there, Lacuna."

CHAPTER 12

The park was different from what Kelisha had described. Firstly, since the season was currently late fall, all of the trees had lost their leaves, minus the appearance of a few remaining ones. The ones that were left were red, contrasting starkly against the white and brown bark of the trees. The aura of fall gave the birch trees a dead sort of look, their slim branches reaching pathetically into the sky as blood red leaves trickled off of them. After taking a short scan of the nearby area, Lacuna and Sonai began their hike towards the guardian's hidden pond.

Trekking past trees for the next couple hours should've been a calming, therapeutic experience, but feeling that way now was impossible. First, they were on the lookout for what could possibly be one of the most dangerous fae known to man. Second, as they passed more and more trees, their brown spots began to seem less random and more orblike. Almost like eyes, watching their every move. Lacuna wasn't sure if it was just a coincidence, or if the work of a fae was present. Either way, the one who would've notified her if such a thing were going on would be Sonai. However, she had been awfully quiet throughout the hike so far.

Breaking the silence, Lacuna asked, "Do you sense any fae nearby?"

"Nah, not yet," she muttered.

"Ok then."

The silence continued for a while longer after that, until the two girls came across a long line of mushrooms. They were all pitch black in color.

Sonai spoke up, mostly to herself. "This is probably the area, but will it lead directly into Melterra or a pocket dimension on the Veil?"

0000 "Didn't Kelisha mention being able to leave the area quickly? Most likely it's on the Veil."

"Gotcha." Sonai took a confident step over the mushrooms. Lacuna followed suit, looking back one final time. Fog slowly permeated her vision as the trees behind her gained some of their own.

As they began the second part of their hike, Lacuna said, "I had no idea that mushrooms could signify entrances into the Veil."

"Honestly I really, really wonder what they actually taught you in that secret Arius society of yours." She looked back at her indignantly.

"We'll, I wouldn't know for sure. I was taught separately from all of the other Arius. She ducks underneath a tree branch. "Furthermore, the secret society you're referring to is known as Revenali. How do you know what an Arius is, that we come from a secret island, but not that the island is called Revenali?"

"The way I learn about stuff just kinda happens like that?" She pushed past a bush. "I don't really know either. I mean, I've fought Arius before, they tell me they're Arius, I kill them and then I just don't end up learning where they came from."

Lacuna's eyes widened. With a hint of wariness, she asked, "I didn't think you were capable of such a task. How many Arius have you killed?"

"Just because I haven't killed you doesn't mean I can't. Anyways, it's around three so far." Sonai strode along, unconcerned with her answer.

Lacuna's pace slowed to a stressed saunter as she muttered, "Oh."

She didn't like the implications behind the phrase *so far*. She was allowing herself to work alongside an active murderer, and it was her duty to get rid of her. But then again, was she even still an Arius? She'd been asking herself the question nearly every day, yet couldn't seem to make her way any closer to the answer. Or, did she simply not like the answer she was coming to? The Feomin girl walking slightly ahead of her already gave her a suggestion. So why was she still denying it?

Distracted by her thoughts, Lacuna failed to notice the way in which the fog thickened around her and Sonai. Eventually, they found themselves standing in front of a large, stagnant pond. It was surrounded by birch trees smeared with eyes. They weren't just strange markings anymore, despite what some could've tried and argued before.

Immediately, Lacuna detached her sword from her hip.

In the pond itself sat a few geese. They craned their necks in the direction of Sonai and Lacuna, eyes dull and gray. Only a couple of them moved along the pond's surface, gliding so gently that no waves were made. These geese couldn't be real.

Ready for battle, Sonai transformed.

And soon after, a shadowy apparition began to appear above the water. Long wispy tendrils emerged from just above where its head should be. Shadows that represented claws extended from the shapes of hands, and the only defined area on the creature was its eyes. Deep, dark blue eyes that attempted to pierce through Lacuna's soul. As the shadow formed more and more, the geese around it slowly began to sink; the oxygen that their false bodies stole bubbled towards the surface. Once the last geese around the creature finally sank, a hoarse voice echoed from across the pond.

"Foolish mortal, thou dare enter my domain?"

"Return the soul shard you took from Tobi!" Sonai commanded the guardian.

"Anything that enters my domain rightfully belongs to me. That nymph should never have entered here."

"It is entirely twisted to claim another being's soul as your own. Kelisha and Tobi wanted to leave, but you wouldn't let them go without harm."

"That is correct, and I plan to do the same to you, mortal." They began to slowly descend onto the water. "All who enter here shall die."

Sonai readied a fireball. "We'll simply take the shard back by force then."

"That shall work fine then sister. If it is a fight that you are requesting." In a split second, the creature was directly in front of Lacuna, their blue eyes boring into her in a way much colder than the way Sonai's did. "Then a fight is what you shall receive."

Lacuna was instantly shoved against a nearby tree by the sheer force of the shadow's body. As she struggled to stand back up, Sonai quickly slid in front of her before lunging at the guardian with two fireballs in hand. They leaped away from the attack, whisking back towards the pond with the grace of a swan. Sonai continued to throw more fireballs at the guardian. They continued to dodge them, whirling on top of the water's surface in a warped sort of waltz.

Lacuna finally made it back onto her feet, shaking her head from the vertigo. Rather than trying to use her swords, she opts to use magic instead, creating balls of energy similar to Sonai's fiery ones. Both girls hurl magic at the guardian, visibly causing them to falter a bit in their demonic dance.

Once they finally gain some proper footing, the guardian lunges at Sonai, their shadow body raising upwards like the hackles of a cat. They proceed to use magic of their own, summoning a shadowed version of a geese to send at Sonai.

She fights against it, albeit scratched by makeshift claws and whipped by wings. Sonai soon finds herself on better footing, incinerating the goose with fire magic.

Unfortunately, it was simply a distraction. As Sonai fought the goose, the guardian had made their way back to Lacuna, reaching at her with shadow magic. For a good minute, Lacuna dodges and counters these attacks fine, switching between using her own magic and her sword. But the guardian manages to get a nasty hit on her, drawing blood. Lots of blood.

The guardian freezes for a brief moment before their eyes dilate in a twisted sense of delight. They tackle her to the ground, craning towards the large cut made on Lacuna's arm. She pushes her sword against their non-existent neck, struggling against the hold.

"Lacuna!" Sonai screamed as she rushed over.

The guardian observed Lacuna's arm emphatically before taking a quick lick at the cut. As they did so, their shadowy form solidified, wild hair falling down towards their shoulders. Luckily, their more opaque body gave Lacuna a surface to push against, forcing the guardian backwards with the force of her kick.

"Zenon..." they murmured while licking their lips.

Lacuna quickly made her way back onto her feet. "What?"

"Does thou knoweth Zenon? It appears thou art both kindred."

"I do not know of a person named Zenon."

Sonai throws another fireball in the guardian's direction. However, they simply raise a hand catching it within a sharp grasp before dispersing its energies. They turned their head towards Sonai in a stiff motion, like a goose. Did that taste of Lacuna's blood make them stronger?

"Does thy mortal not know of their kin, sister?" the guardian asked.

"Yes, and the reason for why that is relates to what we have entered your domain for. Neither of us know."

They turned their attention back to Lacuna. "Had I known you were kin to Zenon, my welcoming would have been more positive. But such prospects cease to matter now."

The guardian reaches towards Lacuna's arm, grabbing it roughly. "Give me your blood." they demanded.

Lacuna shook her head and Sonai stated, "You can not take such a vital resource without her permission, even if it's within your domain."

They ignored Sonai. "If I truly wanted to, I could simply kill you and take the blood. But everything murdered in this domain becomes still. Very still, as still and as rigid as tree bark. The materials flake easily. The blood flakes easily." They licked their lips, that of which were still wavy and shadow-like. "Mortal, it has been centuries since I have feasted on   life blood. Especially the life blood of a half fae." They smiled at her widely, revealing several rows of spindly teeth–a more exaggerated version of the inside of a goose's mouth. "But your body has come bearing gifts for me. Give me your blood, around a liter at least, and I shall allow you to take the soul shard and leave without further harm."

Lacuna looked towards Sonai for answers in this scary situation. And reassurance. Sonai simply mouthed, "*Do what you want to.*"

Lacuna found the comment unhelpful at this time, but she knew what the answer would have to be. She worded her response carefully, knowing that the creature could turn mistakes against her. "You may take only half a liter of blood in exchange for the items and freedom we seek."

"That shall suffice." With shadowy claws, they deepened the cut in Lacuna's arm. She winces and Sonai restrains herself from tackling the guardian, a strange feeling welling up inside her at the sight. In the span of five seconds, the guardian slurps out all the blood that Lacuna offered, making her feel lightheaded.

The guardians form has completely solidified at this point. They were a very dark-skinned, androgynous presence. The shadowy hair that stood straight up originally now fell down in long waves against their shoulders. Their appearance was somewhat reminiscent of Sonai's human form, but less feminine, much colder and extremely malevolent.

They pointed towards the pond. "The shard you seek lies at the bottom. May we meet again soon, Lacuna." Their body began to fizzle away, as they smiled that same, open mouthed, vile smile at her.

As Lacuna held her arm, she was about to question where the guardian had learned her name from before remembering Sonai had shouted that out loud. The two girls were still surrounded by fog, even after the guardian's disappearance. However, Lacuna didn't feel like the birch trees were watching her anymore, their brown spots now reshaped in randomized orders.

"Are you ok?" Sonai asked when she finally got back to her. She looked down at Lacuna's arm, realizing that the scar had mostly healed.

"Yes." She observed Sonai's confused face. "I think the guardian used some healing magic." After sitting for a while longer, Lacuna's previous light-headedness also went away, allowing her to stand up again.

Both girls made their way towards the pond, peering down into the dark, still water. Nothing was visible from the surface. Under normal circumstances, it would be a surprise that no insects could be spotted floating around it, but the area was a pocket dimension after all.

Sonai clicked her tongue. "We were so close before, and now we've hit a dead end."

Lacuna tilted her head in confusion.

"I… uh… can't swim. Plus, this might be a trap. Who knows what's at the bottom of the pond." Her face twisted. "Or if there even is a bottom, like some of the lakes in Melterra."

Lacuna looked down at the lake again. "I can swim," she stated plainly.

"Lacuna, did you not hear me the first time? Even if you can get in, it might be—"

Lacuna suddenly began stripping all of her clothing, throwing them to Sonai.

Embarrassed as she attempted to catch them, Sonai yelled, "And you have a human life span! You could drown!"

Ignoring her, Lacuna dipped one finger in the water. When it came out fine, she placed her entire face in the water, opening her eyes for a second before coming back out.

"Lacuna, stop!"

Taking an extremely deep breath, Lacuna slinked into the cold water, just barely hearing Sonai yell after her.

When Lacuna was eight years old, one of the temple maids had gifted the Oracle a large jar of pickles. While the gift was somewhat gratuitous for someone as important and regal as the Oracle, they kept it for meals that went well with pickles. Like corned-beef sandwiches. Whenever Lacuna found herself in the kitchen, she would look at the jar intensely and wonder what it would be like to swim around in pickle juice.

In the present day, swimming in the guardian's pond might have been the closest experience Lacuna would get to fulfilling the wish of her eight-year-old self. Minus the non-existent smell, the water underneath the surface was a light green and slightly thick, yet still easily movable. It felt disgusting, and remembering that dead geese were technically somewhere in the pond made it all the more gross. However, from what she could see so far, the geese weren't present. Maybe the guardian took them all as they vanished?

Lacuna swam further down, still unable to see the bottom of the pond. She began to worry that Sonai was right, that it was endlessly and neither Tobi nor herself would see life again.

Speaking of Sonai, from outside of the lake, she was panicking. Badly.

"Lacuna!" she called out for the ninth time within that minute. *"Lacuna, get out of there!"*

Unable to physically hear her now, Lacuna continued to swim downward, in slight panic. The smart thing to do would be to immediately swim back, as her oxygen was going to run out soon. But eventually, she saw something. Many things. Thousands of things..

Glowing shards, all of various colors, sat at the bottom of the pond. And Lacuna could hear voices, whispers, screams and cries resounding from every one of them.

"So this is what was being guarded?" She thought.

But how on earth was she supposed to find Tobi's soul shard, and still have enough oxygen to get back up alive?

From above the water, Sonai had been counting. Lacuna had been under the pond's surface for around four minutes already.

"Lacuna!" she called out for the twenty-fourth time.

All in all, her reaction to Lacuna's current absence was disparate. She had met the woman only a few months ago, and said woman had been trying to kill her until just recently. Sonai despised her personality. Lacuna was uncareful, incredibly bold, but extremely boring too; a. A dumb combination, just like her. She attempted to hide her lack of real knowledge behind a calm demeanor and big words. Sonai noticed just how unnoticed Lacuna was by most people, and how she entirely threw herself at issues without a second thought for slim attention. Her actions completely contradicted her personality, always catching Sonai off guard at the hilarious idiocy of someone who claimed to be a certified faerie killer.

But... it was because Lacuna was so hilarious to Sonai that she enjoyed seeing her around. And when she was around, there would be someone looking for her after she got out of class.

Someone who could match her in combat.

Someone who took care of Myco and wouldn't tell the RA.

Someone who sought after her knowledge, making her feel a lot smarter than most would think.

Someone who asked her if she was ok when she couldn't see her fellow fae around her.

Someone she didn't have to hide her fae identity from.

Someone who could actually look her in the eye, in fae form and human form.

Someone who didn't run away when they saw her, but instead ran towards her.

Someone who called her outfits nice.

Someone who said she looked nice.

Someone who said she was pretty.

Ever since Sonai made the decision to enter the human realm nineteen years ago, she was in search of what defined human nature—what made human souls what they were, and defined their power and prestige along the spiritual planes of the Veil. She wanted to fundamentally understand how other fae around her could end up taking a human as their treasure. At one point in her life, the notion seemed nonsensical.

To find the truth, she attended human schools. She conversed with changelings like Ms. Adalim, and weaved her way through a human-esque life. Yet no matter how many humans came and went, she still lacked an explanation for the power of their souls. There was nothing special about them, she thought. Until she met Lacuna.

Lacuna was someone who highlighted one of the main reasons she decided to live in the human realm for so long. Out of all the souls she had come across so far, hers was one of the strangest and most interesting. Someone possessed a soul so interesting to her, that she wanted them to be by her side like a treasure.

But now that someone was currently at the bottom of a pond. A body of water so still that no life grew around it.

And at this point, no life would grow in it either.

"LACUNA!" Sonai wailed, tears welling up in her eyes. *"LACUNA! PLEASE!"* She cursed out this fragment of human etiquette; punished for it as an unusual, subtly stinging sensation settling on her tongue. But maybe the human at the bottom of the lake would appreciate it. "Please…"

She put her head down against the pond's shore, her horns dipping forwards into the water as her tears mingled with it. "Lacuna…"

Sonai continued to lay there, heart heavy, until she felt a vibration. A small vibration against the still water.

And as she looked back up, a faerie came out of the water, her curly black hair flicking back like a dolphin. And that faerie, that human holding a small, glowing shard, was Lacuna Cryoni. The ex-Arius, long lost Olan, and beloved idiot in Sonai heart.

"I found it," Lacuna stated plainly with a deep breath and a smile.

Sonai floats above the water, pulling Lacuna out of it without looking at her. Once she's finally back on dry land, Sonai shakily exclaims, "Are you stupid?"

"I know my choice was reckless, but I managed to retrieve Tobi's soul shard." The two girls proceeded to trade items, Sonai giving Lacuna her clothes back, and Lacuna giving Sonai the shard.

"How do you even know it's Tobi's?" She stuffed it into her pocket.

"I could hear her."

"Wow, it must be those Olan powers then," Sonai stated, trying to sound nonchalant. She still wasn't looking directly at Lacuna, for two very big reasons.

But Lacuna noticed and put her undergarments back on quickly, even despite still being soaked in soul-snatching pond water. At least now she was partially clothed.

"Sonai…"

She tried to wipe away her tears before looking back at her, hoping that Lacuna wouldn't notice any redness in her eyes since they already were that color naturally.

"Sonai, why are you crying?"

"I wasn't crying. I just got water in my eyes."

Lacuna didn't believe her, but decided not to pry further. Instead she simply put a hand on her cheek. Sonai froze for a few seconds, then hesitantly leaned into the touch.

The touch triggered a memory. One from back in first grade, when she and another girl were sitting and talking underneath the small cave of a playground jungle gym. Low on energy Sonai searched fervently for a way to replenish herself. Like most fae her age, she would've heavily preferred something sweet, like candy. Yet the only food sources around were the various children on the playground. *"What would happen if I took blood from her?"* Sonai wondered one second, and then the next, she'd taken it. Like a vampire. And a few seconds after that, the girl was running towards the teacher, tearfully screaming, *"Mrs. Johnson! Mrs. Johnson! Sonai bit me!"* While Sonai doubted that the bite hurt that badly, she was in trouble. A parent had to be called. She didn't have a parent, but she did know a kind changeling who offered to act as her parent time and time again: Ms. Adalim.

The arm that Lacuna touched Sonai with had been the same one that the guardian stole blood from. The scar was essentially non-existent at this point, but a faint line could be made out by Sonai's eyes. The strange feeling she felt before had come back now, and she looked at the line in a mixture of disgust and envy. Lacuna wasn't just a source of energy for other fae to take from. Whatever Sonai and Lacuna were to one another–simply acquaintances or maybe even friends–one thing was certain in her envious faerie mind: she was hers. She had her first. And Sonai didn't want to see something like that happen ever again.

But Ms. Adalim wouldn't be around to remedy the trouble for her actions now.

Wordlessly, Sonai took Lacuna's hand off of her cheek, slowly pulling her forearm towards her mouth. She bit down, just above the line, allowing her fangs to sink into Lacuna's flesh. Lacuna let out a soft gasp, but didn't pull away. Unlike the coldness of the guardian's fangs, Sonai's bite was warm. Very warm. After a couple seconds, Sonai let go, replacing her mouth with her hand to use a quick healing spell of her own over the wound. Still refusing to look at Lacuna fully, she said, "We can get going after you get dressed." She took off her jacket and handed it to Lacuna. "You can use it to dry off."

She then walked towards the trees. And Lacuna, still sitting on the ground half-naked, looked at her arm and wondered what the new, elaborate scar Sonai had just given her meant.

CHAPTER 13

A round two weeks after retrieving Tobi's soul shard, it was now late November in Ohio. As the final leaves fell around Podim University, so did the mental fortitude of many students.

Midterms had arrived.

Despite needing to prepare for upcoming exams and projects, the four girls were already in the process of completing a more personal project: figuring out the final piece of Tobi's recreation ritual.

Much earlier in the month, Sonai and Lacuna had given Tobi back her soul shard. Upon holding it, it shattered instantly, the glittering shards entering her body in an instant. A few minutes later, she was able to transform into her true form as a nymph. All in all, it was a simple and easy process, minus the guardian battle and near death experience for Lacuna.

And on the topic of Lacuna and Sonai, the two girls began to grow closer. Lacuna found herself spending a lot of time with Sonai and Myco in dorm room *135 B*, discussing various concepts regarding fae and their culture. Coincidently, Lacuna's knowledge was even more limited than she thought, finding basic concepts that Sonai could confirm other Arius knew to be a shock.

"So everybody was once separated into two different courts, right?" Sonai stated as she munched on potato chips, sitting on the couch with Lacuna. "There were the Seelie, like Tobi and the Unseelie, like me and the guardian."

"Yes, I've been told this once before."

"Yeah, but now there are no longer two courts. Haven't been for a good… century, I think? But yeah, we've pretty much been combined."

"What? Why?"

"So basically, for like a millennia there was a huge conflict going on between the two courts about a bunch of stuff having to do with humans and claims and territories and all that stuff." She ate another chip. "But then, everyone was like *'ew, why are we as fae basing our existences on the societal woes of humans,'* which I completely agree with by the way, and so—" Myco rolled around on Lacuna's lap, "to calm the realm, the previous king of the Unseelie and the previous queen of the Seelie got married, and had a kid who is now the current queen of the new fae court and my boss basically. And again, terms like Seelie and Unseelie are human made, which is kinda related to why the conflict happened in the first place and why combining the realms through marriage and an heir was so important…"

Sonai's rant about the current royalty structure was more so reiterations of gossip than important news, but it was still shocking to Lacuna.

She enjoyed how Sonai would often force her to question everything she knew previously, allowing her to greatly expand her knowledge in ways that library books couldn't. Albeit, books didn't speak in an ill-mannered tone with their mouths full of food, but it made Sonai's actions all the more real. And that reality was endearing.

In fact, a lot about Sonai was endearing to Lacuna. She had recently come to find out that Sonai was a straight-A student and majoring in biology. It's why, from Lacuna's perspective, she'd often disappear for days on end. So that she could focus. Her academics were quite admirable in Lacuna's eyes. Despite her own interest in learning, her own grades were mediocre at best.

Sonai was also very playful, which appeared obvious. Yet due to being enemies at one point, Lacuna could only interpret her teasing and pranks as intimidation tactics. This was still partially correct in some ways. However, her poking and prodding at Lacuna's lack of information with quick responses gave her a friendly sense of challenge now. She knew that Lacuna was a relatively simple person. Yet she often asked Lacuna what she wanted, even when she already knew what it was. Her unusual actions were refreshing compared to the rather forced kindness of people in Revenali.

The Oracle would never have done that for her.

Sonai had also coincidently earned her title as a powerful fae. The fire she'd used previously were mere tennis balls compared to the beach balls she could actually produce.

"In Melterra, my powers are even stronger," she noted when they sparred in the woods a couple days ago.

The two of them engaged in a little bit of sparring every now and then, with Sonai letting out attacks so powerful they could've killed her if she was serious. But she wasn't. She wouldn't let the blasts kill her, and Lacuna didn't want to kill Sonai either. That decision became final quite recently.

Sonai was also surprisingly caring, despite her rude persona. She spent much of her time watching over animals—mainly Myco—but small birds and mammals that made their way onto campus as well. Much of her attitude towards humans was mainly attributed to her being a fae, from a culture where human versions of etiquette weren't a norm. That being said, the fae did have their own societal norms and customs. They were simply a lot more hedonistic in nature in comparison to humans. It was one of the other things she had told Lacuna about during a previous visit.

"If you don't wanna talk to somebody, then just don't talk. It's simple." This was her reply to the suggestion of ignoring someone's question.

And one of the other things that Lacuna found endearing about Sonai was something she had definitely noticed, but didn't fully comprehend. She knew that Sonai was pretty, but she originally failed to realize that Sonai was absolutely gorgeous. In both of her forms.

Her overall appearance didn't change much between them. Her hair was still a curly black silk down her back and along her shoulders, and her mahogany skin still turned golden in the sunlight. In human form, her brown eyes simply had a hint of red, reflected off the softness of white scleras. Like a carnelian gemstone in the snow. And in Feomin form, her red eyes had a hint of golden brown, reflected off the hypnotizing blanket of black scleras, volcanic in nature. All this, she knew well already.

But Lacuna had also begun to notice the curve of her spine as she bent down to take something off the coffee table. How despite the defined curvature of her hips, her shoulders were slightly broader. The ridges in her horns and the way she wanted to trace her finger along them, as if they were the walls of the temple back in Revenali. The plumpness of her lips and the ephemeral thought of wanting to put her own against them. And as she proceeded to realize more and more stuff like this, until eventually, Lacuna found herself unable to stop staring at Sonai when she walked past.

Was this what people called a crush?

Consequently, the answer to the question had made itself known to Lacuna in the strangest of ways. The reason why Lacuna was in Sonai's room in the first place was because the two of them, Tobi and Kelisha, decided the best place to look for proof of Tobi's existence would be at a mall she went to years ago. Supposedly there was something significant about it in Tobi's mind, thus they were all going to meet at Sonai's room before heading out. Lacuna was pretty early, as per usual. She waited with Sonai, playing with Myco for a bit and watching TV before she remembered the mark on her forearm. During the past few weeks, it became obvious that the mark was not a scar, but a purposeful symbol on her skin. When Sonai finally returned to the living area from grabbing another soda in the kitchen, Lacuna held up her arm to show her.

She looked at her arm in shock as she put the soda on the table. She stood on the opposite side of the table, away from the couch. "Where did that come from?"

"You."

"Nuh uh, I wouldn't mark you!"

"But you did."

Shocked, she questioned, "Did I?"

"Yes you did. In the forest." Lacuna recalled what she just mentioned. "So, what does it mean if I'm marked?"

"It's uh... kind of an old thing. I don't think you'd want to hear about it." She continued to stare at her arm, wide-eyed.

"But if you did it to me, then shouldn't I hear about it?"

Sonai muttered, hand over her mouth as she turned away from Lacuna. "I can't believe I marked her. When the hell did that happen? This is actually insane..."

"Sonai?"

"It means..." her voice cracked as she turned back to Lacuna. "That by fae standards... you've been claimed as... a food source..."

"Are you going to eat me?"

"No! I didn't even mean to mark you, but 'not meaning to mark someone' is literally impossible!"

"Pardon?"

"Marking is a conscious effort. We can't do that by accident." At least, that was what she thought previously.

"If it's not an unconscious choice, and you don't want to eat me, then is it possible that your mark means more than just food?"

Sonai pivoted on her feet for a moment. "Well, the meaning behind a mark can mean a lot of different things for different fae. Some can give humans magic, while others mark people for food like I just said." She tried to think of an example Lacuna would understand. "Kinda like a vampire?"

"Are vampires fae?"

"Yeah."

"Are Feomin similar to vampires?" She was trying to narrow down the possibilities.

"I don't know. I don't know a lot of vampires personally. But like I was saying, even though marks mean different things, they all connect back to one important thing." She looked down, avoiding Lacuna's eyes. "They signify claiming a human as their own, as a resource or as someone they keep company." There was another thing that marks could signify, but Sonai didn't want that thought to become a possibility. At least, she didn't think she did.

"So, am I yours then?"

"Woah, no!" Sonai thought her eyes couldn't get any wider. "No! Uh, definitely not. And actually…" She thought for a moment. "Maybe I marked you 'cause I didn't want another fae to mark you, but didn't realize that happened because I was tired?" The answer wasn't a lie. She was tired and she definitely didn't want Lacuna to get marked by another fae. But marking wasn't something that just happened out of the kindness of one's heart. "Anyway, as long as I don't reaffirm the mark, it should go away in a month." She quickly went back to drinking her soda.

"Oh." Lacuna looked down at her forearm with a sense of disappointment. So her actions in the forest were a mere accident done in an attempt to protect her? There was no meaning behind the feeling of Sonai's lips against her skin?

"Why do you look so upset?" she asked, placing the soda she started to drink back down again.

"I don't think you're being completely honest with me."

"Does it matter? You're not being honest with me either, Lacuna."

A strange tension was held in the air.

She softly contended, "I think it matters a lot, Sonai."

Sonai walked over to the couch. "Why?"

"Because…"

Sonai leaned over her, voice low. "Because what?"

Lacuna leaned back a bit, somewhat cornered by Sonai's gaze. "Because you…" She paused again, observing the way Sonai's eyes held a glint of fire in the same way they did when she was in battle.

Placing both hands on the top of the couch behind Lacuna, Sonai leaned into her space even more. "Because I what, Lacuna?"

Their faces were incredibly close to one another, allowing Lacuna to feel her breath against her face. All of the previously fleeting thoughts returned to her mind at once, and if she leaned just a few inches closer, she might finally be able to satisfy them. Right as it felt like their truths would finally come to fruition, someone loudly banged on the door. Startled, the two girls jumped away from one another.

"Guys, are you here?" called Kelisha.

They had nearly forgotten about today's plans.

After a few minutes of conversing and apologizing to Kelisha and Tobi, because it turned out they had knocked on the door twice before Lacuna and Sonai finally heard them, they all hopped in Kelisha's car.

The drive to the mall was spent mostly in silence. While Kelisha and Tobi's silence was quite comfortable, the inclusion of comments about the scenery here and there, the same couldn't be said for Lacuna and Sonai. Ironically, the both of them had been placed in the back of the four-seat car. Their legs were practically forced to touch one another's. It made Lacuna's heart, which was already beating quickly, palpitate even faster. After what almost happened in the dorm room, Lacuna wasn't sure she could look Sonai in the eye. Did she notice what she wanted to do, what she really wanted to say? As the questions popped up in her mind, Sonai suddenly spoke up.

"Do you think they got a taco spot up there?" her question was asked without stutters, embarrassment, or malice. Perhaps she didn't realize Lacuna's true intentions…

She attempted to keep her voice leveled and suppress the inclinations of her fervently beating heart. "I have no idea."

Eventually, the stalk silence was indefinitely broken by their arrival at the mall itself. The exterior was enormous, with a parking lot that spanned around the entire building. Once they finally stepped inside, around three floors could be seen from their position, various escalators leading towards their heavenly contents. It was as though the world itself could be found somewhere within the wide, yet convoluted halls and their various stores.

"It's just as amazing as I remember…" Tobi states as she looked around in awe.

Kelsha shook her head. "Yep."

"Hey, does anyone see tacos anywhere?"

"I imagine that those would be located in the food court."

"Yeah, but there are places that sell food around the whole mall though."

"According to the map," Tobi held up her phone, showing an electronic map of the store, "The food court is on the second floor. But before we eat, we need to find something to represent my existence, remember?"

Somewhat annoyed, Sonai asked, "Do you have any ideas?"

"I have a few, but I'm not super sure about them. A lot of it's stuff we all thought about as a group."

"Don't worry, I have ideas too!" announced Kelisha.

"But are those ideas actually helpful?"

"What if we split into groups of two?" Lacuna recommended. "Sonai and I could walk around and take pictures of possible locations, while Tobi and Kelisha look in specific places. Then, we can all meet back in the food court at a specific time."

"Well, we would cover more ground that way…"

"That'll work," they eventually all agreed. Soon after, Tobi and Kelisha waved goodbye, promising to meet the other two at 2:30 P.M. in the food court.

She waited until the other two girls were completely out of sight. She turned to Sonai with a suggestion. "If you wish, we could try and find tacos outside of the food court now."

"Wait, did you make up that whole plan just for that?"

"Yes, is that ok?"

Sonai clicked her tongue. "You sure are something, Lacuna…"

"Pardon?"

"Nevermind, let's go." She then took her hand and led them around the first floor.

The two of them had yet to actually find any stores or booths that sold tacos. However, they did manage to find a booth that sold plush toys. Lacuna found herself enraptured by the sight of large dot eyes on top of clashing colors of yarn.

"I would've never guessed you liked stuffed animals?" Sonai stated with a smirk.

"I'm not entirely sure if I do. It's simply that this toy is made in such a fascinating way."

"Do you want one?"

"Perhaps, but the price is listed at fifty dollars. That's too much to spend for someone unemployed like myself."

"Gotcha…Well, I'm not unemployed, so I guess I'll just have to buy it for you." She picked up the plushie Lacuna had been eyeing the most. It was in the shape of a stubby, anthropomorphic ram; fur was a strange swirl of primary colors. Two uneven black horns made of a different but equally soft material sat on its head.

After handing her money to the cashier, Sonai said, "This is payment for letting me search for tacos."

Lacuna hadn't taken the faerie law of equivalent exchange into account. But she didn't forget everything, and therefore, didn't thank her. But she was a human after all, and still wished there was a way to demonstrate her gratitude to Sonai. As she held the plush ram in her arms, she commented, "In books I've read before, outings like this are categorized as dates. Especially when done with beautiful women such as yourself."

Sonai's gaze snapped towards her, surprised. "You think I'm beautiful?"

"Very." She smiled, this time it was the rare, toothy smile she gave back at Deliliah's party.

"Oh wow, um…" She became flustered. "But this isn't a date…" Suddenly, she remembered Lacuna's disappointed expression from back in her room. Then she came to another shocking realization. "Unless… you want it to be?" Her flustered attitude continued to cloud her judgment as she tucked in her lips and puffed out her cheeks. Sonai was grateful that her complexion prevented Lacuna from realizing how much her face was heating up right now.

As Lacuna looked at the unusual facial expression that Sonai made, a strange pressure building up in her throat. The face was unlike anything she had ever seen her make before. And the feeling was unlike anything she had ever felt before either.

Then Sonai turned slightly to the side, still holding the same unusual expression, presenting the final piece needed for the pressure to explode out of her.

Lacuna laughed. The sound was breathy, rustic, crackly, and entirely unheard of before on her tongue. She slapped a hand over her mouth with a quickness reminiscent of the forest guardian's.

"Eugh…" Now it was her turn to make unusual facial expressions.

Sonai's heart flipped at the sound. "Did you just laugh?"

"I did not mean to make such an odd sound."

"It wasn't odd, you're just happy."

"Happy?"

"Now don't tell me you don't understand what happiness is, like you're some kind robot? I just saw you smile like two seconds ago."

"It's not that. There are plenty of times I've been happy. I just can't recall making a noise like that before in my life."

"You've never laughed before?" Sonai couldn't imagine someone like that. In Sonai's eyes, smiling was often an arbitrary response involved in human social culture. But laughing was a relatively involuntary response, that of which was able to be incited by many emotions. And in this case, laughing was specifically related to happiness.

aLacuna had just told her she had never laughed out of happiness before. Was she truly happy at all?

At the thought, a new sense of passion flared within her. Sonai was now dedicated to making the rest of the day enjoyable for Lacuna, desperately wanting to force as many dry, awkward laughs out of her as possible. She grabbed onto her arm and started pulling her farther down the walkway.

With flustered confidence, Sonai exclaimed, "I vow to make today that happiest date you've ever been on."

"But Sonai…" Lacuna looked down at where Sonai had grabbed her arm. Right along her mark. She paused, taking Sonai's hand off her forearm and intertwining it with her own hand. Satisfied, she continued. "This is the only date I've ever been on."

"Yeah, I thought so," she exclaimed confidently, failing to mention that this was also the only date she'd ever been on too.

CHAPTER 14

I n a large clearing sat a mushroom circle, encasing five Arius like sacrifices for a ritual. Rapidly circling around them were dozens of short men with stubby legs, spindly teeth and bulging eyes. They carried a variety of weapons, from real short swords, to makeshift daggers and even simple sticks. Every one of them wore a bright red hat with a painted look, and some were still dripping with a viscous liquid.

But this liquid wasn't paint. It was blood.

Currently, Jordan Mitchels and his unit of Arius were stationed in Sweden, attempting to deal with a large group of the notoriously homicidal fae referred to as Red-Caps. In Revenali, they were categorized as Unseelie fae, level three in terms of power on a scale from one to five, with five being the most dangerous. They were notorious for their bright red hats and relation to Brownies (another small fae species), but unlike their brethren, they were extremely blood-thirsty. This persona is what their name derives from. The hats they wore were dipped into the blood of their victims. In fact, a few corpses of hikers were found in the area once Jordan's unit arrived. They were also incredibly quick. Even with how trained the Arius were, none of them could outrun a Red-Cap.

Thus they all stayed still, watching one another's blind spots. Attempting to leave the circle was impossible due to the sheer size of the Red-Cap hoard. But the Arius didn't want to leave it either. They desperately needed to guard it. The mushroom circle was conveniently the area that the Red-Caps had been coming from, and having humans stand directly inside of it was both preventing more from entering and letting the ones currently out from returning.

"Ready your weapons!" Jordan announced.

The other four members of his squadron took out long-ranged weapons. One had a spear, another a bayonet, another with a hand-gun, and the last with a rifle. Embedded in each of them was a small crystal, similar in color to the ones used on portal gates in Revenali.

After reading his own weapon, a long wired lasso, Jordan yelled, "Fire!"

From all sides, shots were fired into the hoard of Red-Caps. Some were hit, fading away instantly, while others managed to escape deeper into the forest. Under normal circumstances, such as more average fae or a smaller number, the Arius would have dashed after them. But these were Red-Caps, and despite their stubby legs, they were fast. Incredibly fast. And one of the most violent fae known to the organization. Their methods of killing were downright tortuous. Coincidently, both their appearances and actions are reminiscent of pirates in the seventeenth century.

Jordan instructs the group to simply wait until they begin coming back. "For now, we must properly secure the circle."

"It's no wonder so many people have died in this area, there are tons of those things here," stated one Arius as she took a few crystals from her backpack. She readily began placing them parallel to the mushrooms creating the circle.

"I have a theory that this Tear in the Veil might lead to something important in the fae realm."

Suddenly, another Arius speaks up. "Hey boss? I think a level five just appeared." He points towards the distance, as the other members ready their weapons again.

Jordan looks towards the direction pointed in, spotting a bright golden light. He squints his eyes, attempting to identify any other features within the light. He's soon able to make out a humanoid figure. "Arius number three-five-seven, binoculars," he commanded.

"Yes sir." The Arius quickly retrieved binoculars from the backpack in the middle of the circle, handing them to Jordan.

As Jordan zoomed in to get a better look at the figure, he saw a disturbing scene.

They were smiling, mouthing the words, *"Good luck."*

The one who needed luck the most was Tobi, who was currently taking a break from searching to enjoy a meal in the food court with Lacuna, Sonai, and Kelisha.

"Why does it look like that?" Tobi asked, looking at Lacuna's new plush toy.

Finally reunited, the girls each enjoyed various meals. Kelisha had pizza, Tobi simply bought a sweet tea, Lacuna bought a cartoonishly large burger, and Sonai finally got her tacos. Unfortunately, she wasn't able to get them earlier.

"This is simply how he was born."

Sonai roughly swallowed her bite of taco. "What do you mean 'born'? It's a stuffed toy. It was created in a factory."

She turned to her slowly. "I was simply describing him with a sort of metaphor."

"Y'all are arguing over nothing." Kelisha laughed.

"Macunai is not nothing."

"Macunai?"

"I have named him after you and I, Sonai. I added the 'M' in the beginning for Myco, since they look alike."

"That creature looks nothing like my baby, Myco"

Kelisha interjects. "How could you say that to Macunai, he's your baby too."

"What?"

Tobi sighs in defeat. "We were all talking about pizza like five seconds ago..."

"Yes, Kelisha's correct. Macunai is our child Sonai."

Annoyed, she exclaimed, "I should've never bought you that thing."

Lacuna flashed Sonai a small smile then looked down at Macunai's derpy eyes. They glared blankly at nothing in particular, but reflected everything. Lacuna began to realize he reminded her of herself. The reason she wanted him in specific, despite all of the better looking plushies in the cart, was his placement. He was tucked in a corner, covered not by other plushies, but by the railing. It was as though he had been purposefully put there, the owner subconsciously wishing no one would notice him or his eccentricity. As though he were undeserving of a family unlike all the other, more popular plushies that children were taking with them to take care of.

But Lacuna had noticed him, and she would take care of him. She wouldn't let Macunai, the inanimate plush toy, end up like her.

Lacuna hugged Macunai a little bit tighter as Sonai asked, "so Tobi, have you found anything that marks your existence yet?"

Tobi shakes her head. *"When me and Kelisha looked at some of our ideas, nothing really... clicked?"* She took out her phone. "See? We looked at a couple carts around the mall, went into some stores I remembered from the last time I was here and..." She pulled up a picture of a specific store that sold furniture, "in *Hank's Homes*, we looked at lamps and stuff."

"Yeah, this type of stuff definitely wouldn't be super helpful."

"So, did you guys find anything?"

Lacuna held up her plushie and simply stated, "Macunai."

Sonak clicked her tongue before putting her head down roughly on the table, ironically, since it was partially her fault that she and Lacuna found almost nothing for Tobi.

"In all honesty, I don't believe it was a wise decision to look for an item that represents something as important as existence in a mall," Lacuna stated.

"I guess you're right..." Tobi stated as she looked down with defeat. It was the only thing she could think of. But if she didn't find something soon, this would be the end for her. All her years within this universe, gone because of a truth she didn't even realize existed until recently. It was simply how her world worked, filled with hidden dangers on the other side of the Veil.

"Well, a mark of existence for fae could be split between the two realms, right?" asked Kelisha.

"Yeah, but Tobi can't return to Melterra."

"Well, even if her mark of existence is in Melterra, there should be ways to retrieve it even without going there."

"How?" Tobi asked.

"The human and fae realms can't intersect because they're in different dimensions."

"Don't you mean different realms?" Sonai retorted.

"Well, it's both technically. Let's say the human realm is 3D. The fae realm is essentially in 3.5D, except the extra plane needed to be in another dimension lies within their souls. Which is why fae slowly lose power in the human realm and eventually phase back into their own realm after they lose power completely." As Lacuna and Tobi looked at her confused,

Sonai became interested in her ramble. "Like, imagine a 4D object in our 3D plane. You can't and you'll never be able to because there isn't enough room on this plane for a 4D object. Even if there was one within the 3D plane, it wouldn't *look* right. Wouldn't *be* right, which is why faerie's aren't *right* when they're in the human realm."

"I'm having trouble imagining that…"

"Ok then better yet, imagine yourself in a 2D plane. You would be stuck between two walls." She acted this out. "This is what it's like for the souls of fae. Stuck and unable to access their full potential. Their magic. This magic is also what doesn't *look right* in the human world, because the concept of magic–the ability to form something out of *nothing*–completely messes with the fabric of space."

Sonai roughly swallowed a final bite of taco. "So you're basically saying Tobi's mark of existence should be something from both realms that we can't see from this realm? At least, by human standards."

"Yes, at least if I have my ideas right."

"I think I get what you're saying then."

Tobi clicked her tongue sarcastically. "Physics nerd."

The group then sat in silence trying to think of ideas.

"Wait! Tobi, your existence is marked by the fact you won't let anyone take it from you. Your willpower is noticed more than you think!" Kelisha exclaimed. "And since it's always with you, it transcends both realms."

"Huh?"

"Throughout your life, you've had to persevere through a lot. You've ever given up despite seeming like the kind of person who wouldn't have done so already. This is what most people remember you by. At least, I know I would."

Sonai stated, "I agree with that. With all of the time I've spent having to chase after you, it's obvious that you have a lot of willpower."

"I agree as well."

Tobi accepted the compliments happily. "But what could represent my willpower?"

"Kelisha?" Lacuna asked. "What does your bracelet mean to you?'

"A lot. It was given to me by my grandma."

"Why do you let Tobi live inside it?"

Tobi speaks up, "I need a place to recharge my magic energy."

"So that she doesn't phase through the Veil." Kelisha adds.

Lacuna turned. "How badly do you wish to live, Tobi?"

"I want to live until my goals are completed."

"Huh? What goals?" asked Sonai.

"I want to be happy."

"And without the bracelet, you can't do that, am I correct?"

"... yeah?"

"Obviously? Since she can't live in the human realm without—" Sonai blinked, sighed, then smacked her head against the table animatedly. She gestured to the bracelet as she got back up. "Oh my god! So the answer was right under our noses the entire time? Of course Tobi's mark of existence is literally the thing that allows her to exist at all!"

Tobi thought about Sonai's statement for a second before bursting into laughter. "Wow... we're kind of dumb, aren't we?"

Sonai's animated attitude stopped. She jeered, "Nah, just you."

"Kelisha's bracelet," Lacuna announced, bringing back the group's focus. Kelisha looked down at her arm with a hint of sadness. Not because she feared losing it during the ritual, but because the solution to help her friend was directly attached to her this entire time but somehow didn't realize it. She had been the one suggesting that Tobi should go to the mall they visited all those years ago. Yet the trip only wasted their time. She felt like an idiot.

"My bracelet..."

After finishing their meals, the girls return to Podim University, contemplating when to complete the ritual. Kelisha wouldn't lose her bracelet, but its significance to Tobi's life would increase exponentially.

The next day, the girls returned to the forest by May's Cafe and set up everything for the ritual. Sonai had drawn out the magic circle in an unknown substance, a dark reddish color. Had it been blood, Lacuna would've questioned where she managed to get so much of it.

Tobi was placed in the middle of the circle, in full nymph form, holding Kelisha's bracelet tightly with both hands.

Outside of the circle, Kelisha was soon to make a contract of her own with Sonai. Sonai was also in full fae form, holding a thin stone tablet. She had pricked a finger, placing the blood atop the tablet. Kelisha had done the same. "Before we begin," she stated, "as a witch, mage, and or practitioner of magic, you must vow to never reveal what you might hear today to another fae, or Tobi once she is remade. If you do, you will be killed instantly. Do you understand?"

"Yes. As a practitioner of magic, I vow to never let the secrets revealed during today's ritual escape my tongue. If they do, may the rest of my life blood run along with this drop." Another drop of blood fell on the tablet.

As Kelisha and Sonai began taking their places around the circle, Lacuna looked at Tobi in the middle. During this short period of time, her relationship with Tobi was somewhat akin to friendship. It was nothing like the current, strange relationship between her and Sonai, but the two of them also weren't super close either; unlike how she was with Kelisha. It made her kind of sad that she wouldn't be able to bond with her over *Eternal Wood*. But she doesn't let it show.

However someone else did, letting every emotion they felt for their one and only familiar escape just like she did from Melterra. Tobi's best friend, Kelisha, was currently shaking from her spot outside the circle.

"Tobi..." she whimpered, trying to hold back tears.

Tobi attempted to reassure her. "Kelisha, it's going to be ok."

"Before the ritual begins, it's time for you to fulfill you end of the deal Tobi." Sonai's voice became militant. "What is the Olan?"

Tobi took a deep breath. "From what I've gathered, the Olan—" she pointed at Lacuna, "she is a symbol of destruction for the universe. A half-fae born from the courtship of Queen Titania and a powerful human."

And as Tobi said this, Lacuna realized something. "The union between the queen of fae and a powerful human... a near perfect union, depending on the human." She kept this thought to herself. "That's what the Oracle was talking about."

Sonai, the usually confident fae, was shocked. "The queen had a child with a human? As in, the current queen? Daughter of the union between the two courts?" She turned towards Kelisha and Lacuna. "Do y'all understand how powerful the half-fae child would be? Lacuna, do you understand how strong you could be?"

Kelisha looked at her somberly. "Wait, since you're the child of the faerie queen, does that make you a princess?"

"Lacuna does have a princess-like aura to her if I'm being honest." She stared closely at her. "I can kinda see her resemblance to the queen now." Sonai laughed, half out of shock and half out of finding the situation to really be funny.

Lacuna fell to her knees, distraught. She's not just part fae, she's a faerie princess essentially. She feels disgusted. But why? She thought she got over that already. Sonai and Tobi are fae, and she's fine with them. In fact, where does her hatred of fae come from? Simply because of previous teachings, that the fae were tricky and wicked? And despite these teachings being presented by a person, an island who kidnapped her? Lacuna felt extremely unsure of herself. But has she ever truly been sure?

Suddenly, she felt a hand on her shoulder.

"Are you ok?" Sonai asked.

"I'm not sure." With a sigh, she recollected herself out. "But that doesn't matter right now. We can discuss all of this more later." She then looked at Tobi, a feeling different from her initial shock fueling her body. "Tobi, thank you."

"Huh?" she questions, repulsed by the words. "That's simply my part of the deal. Please don't thank me."

"You have provided me with the knowledge I've wanted to know my whole life. The truth. You were a good friend, even in the short time that I've known you. If I'm still here in Podim, Ohio after all of this, I'll make sure to treat your new self kindly." She smiles. "That, I promise."

Kelisha suddenly rushes into the circle, hugging Tobi tightly. "I'll never forget you, any version of you. When you come back, I'll take even greater care of you." Tears start falling from her eyes. "I'm going to make up for any time I've been mean to you, or inconsiderate, or lazy. You were one of the best friends I've ever had. And even though it's my bracelet that's a physical representation of your existence to the world, the fact that this version of you once existed will always stay within my heart."

"Kelisha…" Tobi was crying now too. "I'll never forget you, I won't allow it." She hugged her even tighter.

They say a few final words as everyone gets back into position. The three girls raise their hands, letting the magic energy flow from them onto Tobi. Tobi begins to sparkle brightly, and as the light becomes brighter and brighter, she looks at Kelisha one final time to say, *"Goodbye…"*

Then the light exploded.

But beyond that light, was the light of another fae, one who watches all, and wants everything as well.

Derived from a being who knows existence as nothing but the creation of all things beautiful. The child of the queen of fae, Zenon, watched this ritual happen. After it was finished, they whisked themselves back into Melterra with a mere twirl, appearing within the trunk of the Great Tree in seconds. They sauntered towards the very middle, placing themselves before the queen.

"Sonai has taken matters into her own hands."

"As I expected."

"You know, there was someone with her, and her aura was incredible. It almost reminded me of you, mama. Do you know of her?"

The queen flaps her wings for a second, gusts of wind flowing throughout the room. "Yes, most likely." She said nothing else.

Zenon sighs, "fine, keep your secrets then. The Red-Caps in the north have been dealt with by fae hunters. The rebellion will soon be squashed."

She was not entirely satisfied by their response. "It will not be that simple, my child. There are many, many factors associated with the rebellion and its allies. We mustn't leave such conflicts to fae hunters."

"Hmm, I guess…" Zenon scoots one foot along the bark. Soon after, they begin to dance around, swinging to an absent melody. "I best take my leave." They giggle, flying out of the tree.

The queen doesn't reply to this. Instead, she stands and walks over to a large hole carved out of the tree. She looks out at Melterra, but wonders at nothing in particular. Exactly as she had done for millenia.

CHAPTER 15

I t had been over a week since Lacuna learned the truth of her existence. It had also been a week since she was supposed to meet Jordan for another monthly check-in; she never went.

He sent her a text, asking where she was. She didn't reply.

He tried to call her. She didn't pick up.

What she did do however, right before the meeting day, was write down the numbers of all her friends, buy a new phone, then destroy the old one.

Physically, the action was useless; mostly symbolic. After all, he knew exactly where she was. It would simply be a matter of time until Jordan, or perhaps the Oracle's own forces, would come to retrieve her. Or confirm if she was dead.

After the ritual was completed, Tobi had transformed into some sort of egg, entangled in a chain that had once been Kelisha's bracelet. No one knew when she would hatch, not even Sonai. After cleaning up the area, Kelisha shakily picked her up, gently placed her in her backpack, then went on her way with many *goodbyes*, *thank yous*, and *I'm sorrys*. These were mostly meant for Lacuna, as Sonai cringed heavily near the end of their short conversation.

Speaking of Sonai, she was preparing to head back to Melterra now that her mission with Tobi was complete. But only for a little bit, since she still had a college degree to obtain.

The prospects of Sonai's college education had Lacuna thinking more deeply about her own. She was only here at Podim University in order to hunt down Sonai. She enrolled as a General Studies student simply because there was nothing else that she wished to do, or would've had time to do. Even before college, she was never even enrolled in an official high school or middle school. She was essentially "home-schooled" her entire life. And even all of that was lies, just like her current college life.

Lacuna had been spending even more time deconstructing her previous beliefs about the two realms. About Revenali. About Marcus's message. About the Oracle, who despite leaving a hole in her heart from their lies and betrayal, never truly bonded with her due to their neglect and vague behaviors. The conflicting feelings left Lacuna in a new sense of emotional pain.

The expansiveness of human emotions, sometimes influenced by fae. So was it truly fae that created pain within this world as Marcus said? If so, then she was pain. And humans got rid of pain. But she was also created to get rid of pain herself; being the child of the faerie queen and a human made her powerful. Her soul was powerful. It gave her the ability to stay on the human side of the Veil without using magic. This would have been helpful in defeating Feomin like Sonai, yes, but Lacuna was sent out without any experience. It was extremely stupid, and she was surprised she didn't realize how stupid it was before. In fact it was so dumb that it seemed purposeful. What's the point of sending out an inexperienced Olan Arius to defeat a Feomin? Just to see if it was possible? To test her power level? The questions simply continued to pile up within her mind.

But as she continued to increase her time spent with Sonai, very few questions felt as though they were alleviated.

"Your existence would have to be some sort of scandal in the court. The royal family is of pureblood fae royalty and has been for centuries. All children born from the queen are immediately considered royalty, and usually have to remain in the Great Tree until they hit a certain age. But since you're not a pureblood fae, you were abandoned. It gets even worse, since the current queen's existence is already considered to be so scandalous since she's mixed between Seelie and Unseelie." She paused to change the TV channel. "This is what I meant when I said you gotta be pretty powerful." Then she chuckled, "I wonder who the lucky human is... or was."

Despite how often Lacuna thought about her mother and the concept of having parents, it was rare that she thought deeply about her father. To think of a parent interacting with her, ruffling her hair–the image of a father figure didn't appear immediately like a motherly one did. What he might look like, his relationship with her mother, who happened to be the faerie queen? How similar to him did she look? How similar to the queen did she look, actually?

As Sonai was getting a few things situated for Myco before her trip, Lacuna sat on the couch, flipping through more TV channels. Sonai perked up suddenly, turning to Lacuna and asking her, "Have you ever wanted to go to Melterra?"

"Hmm?" As she hummed out the response, she thought about it for a moment. There had been times, fleeting thoughts of being snatched by fae like she heard in stories. However, unlike the stories, at the end of her fantasies, she didn't end up joining the fae or growing miserable. Instead, her daydreams would end with her successfully mutilating the otherworldly beings and escaping whilst covered in blood and pixie powder. "Perhaps. Why do you ask?"

"I don't know, I'm kinda in the mood for some trouble. If you suddenly appeared, I'm pretty sure Melterra would be in chaos for a little bit. Plus, you'd finally get to meet the queen."

"That would be interesting. In all honesty, I've been thinking about my current life a lot. I've come to the realization that there's nowhere else I can really go, so I wouldn't mind, depending on what happens going forward."

As the thought settled in Lacuna's mind, the more intrigued she became. Rather than sitting on the vague answer she gave before, she stated, "Yes, I would like to visit Melterra, and perhaps, stay there permanently." It was time for her to be remade in a way similar to Tobi, just not physically.

Soon after this conversation, the two girls made their way towards a forest near Podim, one that Lacuna hadn't seen before. Deep within it was a ring of mushrooms, all white and pearlescent. Right before stepping inside, Sonai grabbed Lacuna's hand and said, "Focus," as she closed her eyes and held a hand over the circle. Lacuna followed suit. Together, the interior of the ring produced a large pillar of light that glowed like a star. Slowly and gently,

Sonai led Lacuna into the light. She gave her a small smile. Is this what it felt like to be snatched by fae? If so, perhaps Lacuna would have succumbed to the charms and glamour of the Veil's fae a lot sooner.

Upon exiting the portal in Melterra, Sonai was instantly transformed into her Feomin form, but something about her was much brighter, more ethereal. Her darker pallet contrasted beautifully against the forest of exotic purple flowers and wisteria-esque trees they arrived in. The fiery aura of her eyes appeared to grow too, appearing more wild and free in their original environment underneath the misty, cool sky.

She floated high into the sky in an instant motion, before coming back down just as quickly. "I'm gonna have to teach you how to fly."

"Is that even possible for me to do?"

"There are some fae that can't, but since you're the queen's kid, you should have the ability to. It's gonna be helpful for getting around in general. Especially to the top of the Great Tree."

"Well, how do I start?"

Sonai took both of Lacuna's hands into her own. "First you have to focus your energies around your body. It should be easier here, since magic is enhanced in Melterra. Simply think about how it would feel to fly, and you can do it. It should be kinda like swimming through air." She chuckles, "But I wouldn't really know that 'cause I can't swim."

Lacuna held onto Sonai's hands tightly as she shut her eyes. She thought of these moment in the guardian's pond, the force of her body sliding through the water. The power of Sonai's own magic as she pushed her along. And how she was here, even now, to ground her.

"Ahh you're doing it!" Sonai announced.

Lacuna opened her eyes and realized she was around twelve feet off the ground; she stopped herself from panicking, making sure to keep her focus. Soon enough, she managed to push herself in different directions. Yet she still hadn't let go of Sonai's hand. This quickly changed, as she eventually let go, walking on air as if it were freshly mopped linoleum floors. Sonai followed close behind, and it was very much appreciated by Lacuna.

Suddenly a large, draconic bird flew above them in the sky, spooking Lacuna. She began to fall, but Sonai caught her.

Lacuna laughed from embarrassment, and Sonai was delighted. She knew that some fae fed on human laughs, and although she had never been one of them, Lacuna's could probably persuade her to be. They tried flying for a little while longer, Lacuna letting Sonai hold her hands more closely. As she got the hang of it, the two began to waltz in the sky as practice for movement. The dizzying spins led captivating stares at one another, until they both ended up back on the ground, slightly tired and invigorated by the other's care and magic power. And as the two girls looked back at each other, happy and free, one leaned in and kissed the other. And the other gladly kissed her back.

Eventually the two flew further into the realm, passing the forest of wisteria and arriving in a meadow full of golden foliage. Fae of various shades of blue, yellow, and peach-orange skipped around chatting. Some, younger in appearance, were running around playing tag, while a few others who seemed more mature were creating flower crowns from the flowers on the ground.

"The Summer Court mainly meets around here," Sonai noted while pointing to a beach a few yards away, the sand a similar color to the meadow. "After we talk to the queen, I'll try to show you around all of the other courts and unclaimed areas."

Lacuna looked around the Summer Court in awe. Such a rich environment. Were all places in Melterra like this? If so, then why would fae ever want to come to the human realm? So much of the nature there was destroyed or polluted, nowhere near as fresh and vibrant. As Lacuna continued to wonder, a few of the Summer Court tilted their heads to look in her direction. As they stared at her, Sonai grabbed her arm, leading her away.

"They're starting to sense your aura. Let's wait to meet other fae until the queen sees you first."

"Or else what?"

"Some might just crowd around, but others might try to fight you."

Beyond the golden fields was a large river. It separated a normal looking forest with spruce-like trees from the rest of the realm. Despite the height of the trees, the forest appeared extra canopied, with little light shining through. As Sonai and Lacuna flew over the river and made their way deeper into the woods, the sight revealed was unlike anything Lacuna had ever seen before.

Before her was a tree, gargantuan in size. Its trunk reached far beyond the misty sky, reminiscent of the pillars that the portal gate in Revenali was made of. The few branches that came from the truck had a similar type of width, yet obviously, still not comparable to the size of the truck. Its leaves, although mainly green, also contained speckles of various rainbow colors. Like the colors of dark opal. Vines made their way towards the ground, as a few massive leaves did as well. And upon closer inspection, Lacuna realized that various fae were riding said leaves.

"Welcome to the Great Tree, previous home to the queen of the Seelie Court, and current home to the queen of the New Court." With a smile she said, "So, do you want to fly straight up, or ride on a leaf?"

"I still don't trust my abilities enough to fly..." She looked up, trying to see the tree's top, "...that high. If riding a leaf would be easier, then I would prefer that option."

"Gotcha. Let's get going then." She led her towards a yellow leaf that had fallen recently. It was around the size of a medium swimming pool; slightly curved in the illusion of one too.

Upon sitting inside it, her legs crossed, the leaf was immediately lifted into the air. Lacuna hung onto Sonai, making her laugh.

As they rose higher and higher, the land of Melterra became more visible. Lacuna could see the Summer Court, the Wisteria forest, other seasonal courts, and a few other unnamed areas. All of these places illuminated the world in a kaleidoscope of colors that matched the tree. She looked behind her and saw more large winged creatures in the far distance, some bursting through ocean water and rising to heights in the sky that Lacuna was unsure the leaf could reach. And as she looked into the sky, eventually passing over the clouds that gave it a misty look, and pushing through a cool breeze that smelled faintly of lavender, the leaf stopped at a large branch. Upon getting off of the leaf and standing on the branch, Lacuna looked up again,

"Right now, we're a little bit too high, so we're gonna have to follow the branch towards the center and float down a little bit."

"Why did the leaf take up this high then?"

"The leaves of the Great Tree can only make their way back to their original location. They're stuck in this permanent cycle type of thing. Anyways, it doesn't take long to get to one of the tree floors, so don't worry."

The two walked along the branch carefully, even despite its large diameter. Additional leaves continued to fall off as a few others came back up, transporting a couple fae from various courts. Lacuna looked at other branches, observing the same situation occur. Everyone was making their way to the center of the tree. At the end of the branch, Lacuna peered down into the trunk, taking in its equally massive interior. The walls were like honeycomb, each uneven shape crevice filled with furniture and other fae. Additional pillars and ledges extended from other parts of the tree. Various wooden trails went between all of the areas. Fae bustled back and forth like busy market vendors, discussing things in various languages. A few of them, Lacuna could understand from her education as an Arius, but the conversations were about topics that Lacuna was unsure she'd ever hope to understand. She wondered how one would be able to find the queen amongst all of the chaos.

Sonai took her hand and stated, "Get ready." They began to float down as a few fae looked at them. The quickness of their descent prevented any further inspection. Sonai took her towards a large mirror-like hole at the far end of the tree trunk. It glowed in waves like opal. They entered it, and on the other side was a massive throne, which sat a beautiful winged woman similar in size.

This woman, the Queen of Fae, went by many names: Titania, Gloriana, Una, Mab, etc., although none had any real meaning to her. She was a large presence, both physically and spiritually. Her wavy black hair, which reflected light like crow feathers, reached down far to the floor and pooled around her feet. Her skin was lighter in color, yet even by human definitions, couldn't necessarily be described as that of a specific region of the world. However, her features—evidently fae in nature, but still humanoid—held the aura of an ancient being. They were reminiscent of a human who was one of the first to exist.

Above her was another faerie. They had a very similar complexion but their hair colors differed. An afro of hair sat wispy on top of their head as they twirled around the throne before stopping abruptly to look at Lacuna and Sonau with a wave.

"Lacuna," her voice boomed throughout the area as if the tree's interior were a cave. "You have finally arrived." She held out her hand expectantly.

"Your Majesty," Sonai announced, "the fugitive has been dealt with."

"I already know of it, Sonai. I now wish to speak with the guest you brought here." She looked at Lacuna with her golden brown eyes. They looked as though they were always bathed in sunlight. "My daughter."

Hearing the woman she'd never seen a day in her life refer to her as *'daughter'* made Lacuna feel conflicted. She'd originally believed that mother and child were supposed to have an instant connection between them upon being united, whether it was at birth or asasasasasa years later. But Lacuna was unable to imagine the queen ruffling her hair like Reno's mom did, nor could she imagine her giving advice and instructing her with minimal affections like the Oracle did. Or perhaps, the reason she couldn't imagine these things is because she had never wanted the chance.

Without manners or introductions, Lacuna asked, "Did you abandon me?"

"My dearest Lacuna, I never abandoned you."

"How?"

"It's quite simple, honestly; I made a deal. For the safety of my offspring, I gave someone the power they desired. You just so happened to be the power."

Lacuna thought about her words for a moment. "So then… you gave me to the Oracle for a deal?"

"It was entirely for your safety. You wouldn't have been safe here in your younger years living here in Melterra."

"But how was I safe with the Oracle? I wasn't given any knowledge about the beings that make up my supposed homeland. I nearly made wrongful contracts with numerous fae. The lack of education that the Oracle provided nearly killed me." She lowered her voice. "Honestly, why did you even have me if existing in this world was so dangerous?"

The queen sat silent for a moment before smiling down at her. "Come closer Lacuna, and I shall present you with the truth."

Lacuna approached the throne in stifled strides. Once she was just in front of the queen, she shrunk, making herself a height more comparable to Lacuna's own. Then, she held out her hand, ushering Lacuna to grab it. And before she did so, the queen said, "Your father. You are in this world because I wished to keep your father in this world."

As she squeezed Lacuna's hands gently, she closed her eyes and began speaking in a language the Lacuna couldn't comprehend. And soon after, her mind was filled with the color of opal.

CHAPTER 16

A ureo spent many of his days in solitude. Slumbering upon abandoned beds, their previous hosts long gone from the earth. Taking experimental elixirs for his migraines and incessant pains, brewed by professionals who seldomly worked in the asylum. Some came and went, others permanent fixtures in his melancholy called life.

Wolfgang Hospital was a small building, slightly worn down and vine covered. Although it wasn't abandoned, the hospital had little funding, and few people visited in need of medical assistance. The town of Padalo, Iceland had few residents in and of itself, yet there were better hospitals available in the area, with better funding and materials.

Throughout the years, Aureo questioned why he was still here.

It was always possible for him to move to a different hospital, but he had yet to try. Perhaps his resistance was due to an odd mix between money troubles, a lack of family and not wanting to abandon his one and only friend, named Denando, who lived with him in the ICU. Perhaps it was also due to Wolfgang Hospital being one of the few to attempt to cure his illness. Back when the hospital was more notorious, its laboratory system and medical research practices were sought out by various doctors who strove for greatness. Yet as other hospitals in the town grew, and Wolfgang was left behind, so too was its medical research.

Even so, there were a few doctors that stayed. One of which was Dr. Angela Wilkins, an infectious disease specialist and immunologist. She was mainly stationed in the ICU with Aureo and Denando, spending her days trying to determine if Denando was getting better and if the fifth new medication Aureo had received that month was working.

"Good morning Mr. Cryoni," she said to Aureo. "How are you feeling today?"

"Fine. Same as usual," he said simply.

Soon after, one of the nurses who was always present came over, performing a basic health checkup and telling Dr. Wilkins the information. As it happened, Aureo stared at the white concrete walls, badly wishing to leave the stagnant environment, at least for a moment.

Dr. Wilkins asked him a few questions, her words droning on as she asked him the same questions she always asked, coming to the same conclusions as she always came to.

"Based on how you feel right now, I'm afraid the medication may not be working. However, we're gonna run a few blood tests just to be sure." She smiles. "Did you know we're getting a few systems updated? They should allow us to detect any further health defects sooner."

"Well, that's good."

"Yeah that sounds great!" exclaimed Denando a couple beds over. "Did the hospital order any new beds, because these ones are getting stiff!" He chuckled lightly.

"I'm afraid not, Mr. Galvin, but if needed, I can get a nurse to bring you some more pillows and fresh sheets."

"That works too, I guess."

"Ok then, I'll be back for your check up in around thirty minutes Mr. Galvin." She turned back to Aureo. "Mr. Cryoni, your results should be ready by tomorrow. Please have a wonderful day."

"You too, Dr. Wilkins."

"Bye, Mrs. Wilkins!"

Then the day went on as usual. They ate breakfast, talked about nothing important, and then Denando took his usual afternoon nap. His naps often lasted hours. He'd sleep for two, eat a quick lunch, then resume sleeping for five. As he snored, another nurse would be typing away in the background. What she could've possibly been writing in the nearly empty hospital that was Wolfgang, Aureo had no idea. Perhaps she was filling out new job applications.

The sounds drove Aureo crazy. He'd try to listen to something different, like the sounds of birds cawing from the slight ajar window. Or he'd put his head against the plush cloth of his pillow, straining to hear the sound of conversation as devices beeped on the second floor. It worked, sometimes. But after a while, those sounds also became repetitive, adding to his worsening state of happiness.

He needed to get out of here, at least for a moment.

Aureo grabbed his cane sitting beside his bed. With somewhat stiff legs, he hobbled towards the exit of the ICU.

"Bathroom sir?" The nurse asked.

"Yes," he stated simply, pressing the button for the automated door.

It was always odd to Aureo that the ICU didn't have its own bathroom area. While this wasn't entirely a problem for Denando, as he used a catheter due to being bedridden, Aureo's case was a different story. But luckily, that might work in his favor today.

He made his way towards the elevator furthest down the hallway. There was one right in front of the ICU, so most doctors didn't use the far one, which happened to be closest to the bathroom as well. It gave him a greater chance to avoid being caught. Outside of the unit, the third floor of Wolfgang was made up of offices, with many being unused due to lack of staff.

No music played on the elevator as it shakily descended to the ground floor. Aureo looked out carefully before leaving out of an exit door nearby. There were no security measures taken to protect this door. Beyond it was a courtyard with many benches and wilting flowers. A few yards beyond that was a small wooded area that looked down upon the lower floors of Wolfgang hospital from a small hill. While Aureo could walk, going up a hill—even one the mere height of the one nearby—could possibly be like climbing a mountain for him. But despite his mind's protests, his heart's wishes pushed him towards it. Thus his legs, that became ever so slightly less stiff from the beginning of his hike, strode towards the mountain. He hoped the only being who might be looking at him from above was the birds.

He managed to scale the hill quicker than he thought, and with only slight fatigue. If he found a nice rock nearby, he'd sit down there. And he managed to find one quickly; a large, unevenly shaped stone sat before a ledge that overlooked Wolgang hospital from a different angle, deeping into the woods. Aureo sat down, tasting the dryness of his mouth, observing the building's decrepit stone covered in vines, feeling the breeze on his skin, and catching the scent of grass.

And then behind him, he heard something. Someone.

She approached him slowly, floating in an attempt to lessen the pressure she left behind, even despite sitting on the Veil in the current moment. The man did not turn around to look at her, but she knew he could sense her. Somehow. Was this truly a human she was observing?

"The weather is beautiful this afternoon, right?" he asked his unknown visitor.

"Yes, I agree."

The man turned his head, locs swaying hypnotically, to look at the woman behind him.

And the woman, winged and clad in otherworldly beauty, looked directly into the human man's lavender eyes. Yet he had no reaction.

"Hello?" they both said in unison.

Aureo peered up at her curiously. "You're... not from around here, are you? Are you one of the neighbors from the Otherside?"

She contemplated his question for a moment. "Yes, you could say that. I'm surprised that you can see me right now. Most humans are unable to look at those of us sitting on the Veil."

"I know. It's strange to me too. But, for some reason I've always had the ability to see the Otherside."

"How interesting. Can you tell me more?" She then floated beside him, rather than behind him.

Aureo spoke with the mysterious faerie woman for a while, the exact amount of time unknown to him. His conversation with the woman was enjoyable, filled with questions about concepts Aureo knew well, yet had never been asked about before. His ability to see the fae, even when they weren't physically standing in the human realm, was referred to as Veil Sight by the woman.

"It's a gift, and you should cherish it," she said. Her comment made Aureo smile.

Aureo knew he needed to return to Wolfgang soon. He feared hospital staff discovering this area, banning him from coming in out of worry for his health. But would it really matter though? He was in a strange state of limbo regarding his disease. Never getting better, yet luckily, not becoming worse. At least, for now.

Eventually, he left, waving goodbye to the non-corporal faerie woman.

"I'll try to see you again someday. Maybe next week?"

"After seven moons?"

He counted the days in his head. "Yeah, after seven moons." He smiled at her.

She didn't smile back. But that was ok.

For the rest of the week, Aureo excitedly awaited the next time he could meet the woman. If Denando noticed his improved mood, he didn't say it.

So as the days went on, and the moon was replaced by the sun, she waited. Patiently for the man with violet eyes, dark skin, and a head full of long locs. Now, she didn't just stand in the forest and stare at the hospital. That was impossible. Just like the man who's name she didn't ask for, she also had a designated place to be. In Melterra, she had various duties. And although she had yet to be crowned queen, as the offspring of a newly remade monarchy, she was never supposed to leave in the first place.

After exactly seven moons, the man returned. He walked towards her, eyes first, with a smile and a wave. And then they talked some more, just like they did before. About the forest. About animals. About the sun and the moon and the stars. About the universe. About life.

And their talking continued for many more moons after that. She eventually lost count. Even after all these moons passed. She still never learned his name. Or why he was locked away in the strange decaying building. Until today, coming to the conclusion that she should just ask him rather than wait.

"Human, I have had yet to ask this, but do you have a name?"

"It's Aureo." He felt no fear at the thought of her holding his fate. "How about you? What's your name?"

"I… don't have one. Not yet. I am to receive one once I'm queen."

"Queen… you never told me you were royalty?"

Without pause she retorted, "You never told me your name. You have also never told me why you live there." She pointed to Wolfgang hospital.

"Ok, I guess that's fair." He stayed silent for a moment. "The building there is a hospital. I live there because I'm sick."

"How sick?"

"…Very sick." He tapped his cane.

"How so?" she tilted her head.

"I have an illness that no one else has heard about. So rare that I got to name it."

She looked at his eyes, like she always does. "I've been wondering this for a while, but are you part-fae perhaps?"

"It's unlikely. Wouldn't you have sensed that yourself, like you've told me you can before?"

"There could be hidden cases."

"Would that explain my illness?"

"Possibly."

Silence continued once again.

"Um… as you said earlier, you don't have a name yet, right?"

"That is correct."

"Would you mind if I gave you a name?"

A name given to her by a human? Blasphemy for a fae from a lineage such as her own, but she couldn't resist the excited glance of his violet eyes.

"You may choose a name for me. However, it shall be more of a nickname than anything due to spiritual reasons."

"Ok, I completely understand." He looked upon her corporal form, one that she had been using more often now, sitting in the human realm with him rather than along the Veil. He observed the glow of her skin under the sunlight, how her golden eyes gleamed brighter from its rays. The shimmer of her hair as it refracted the greens, pinks and purples on its dark background. He took in her strong features and their allure, wondering if she had any statues built of her yet on the Otherside. If she didn't, he hoped that in his next life, he could have the ability to build at least one for her.

"Endora," he stated confidently. "I think your name should be Endora. It means light in Greek."

"Endora…" she let the name rest on her tongue. "I like it."

"And I like you."

Endora tilted her head.

"You may take my statement in any way that you personally wish to infer it." He smiled at her before turning his gaze to Wolfgang Hospital. Then the two, Aureo and Endora, sat in comfortable silence again.

But silence wasn't always comfortable.

A few weeks worth of moons later, Endora waited by their usual ledge of the woods, waiting to see if Aureo would come. He did of course, he always did, but something was different. He hobbled on his gain with more support. He waved with no smile. And when he sat on his rock, he didn't ask Endora, "So, what do you wanna talk about today?"

Instead he sat in silence. A deafening, sad silence that muted all the colors of the forest. Especially the violets.

"You are upset, I believe?" Endora asked.

"Denando died last night." He did not turn to look at her.

"Ah. That does seem unfortunate for you."

He knew the connotations of her comment were not meant out of malice. She did have little reason to care about Denando. She never met him, and neighbors from the Otherside were not often attached to the concept of death. But it's what made her reaction to Aureo's next comment all the more somber.

"I'll be joining him soon." He tapped his cane rhythmically against the rock.

"Why?"

"My doctor, Wilkins, the one I told you about before, finally got her new blood testing machine. It turns out there had been defects in the transcription process of the old one, so now the hospital's discovered that my illness is much more severe than they thought." His voice lowered. "Turns out, I only have two months left to live. And in the one month period, I might not be able to walk anymore."

"Aureo…" There was nothing she could say to him. No *sorry*, or *it's going to be ok*, would suffice. That was a concept she knew since the day she was born. But she did want to do something for him, for the man who talked with her about her escapades, who's understanding of the universe would enrapture even the most brilliant of fae scholars. A man who lived a life of philosophy, even despite that life being restricted to hospital beds and woodland. For the man who gave her a name: Endora, and who would be the only being in existence to ever call her by that name.

There was little she could do. She couldn't heal nor take him to a healer on the Otherside. His human body, especially in its weak state, would likely not survive. Likely he would be remade slowly, or she could remake him instantly, but who knew what would happen there? He could lose all of his memories, or be transformed beyond recognition. And Endora liked Aureo the way he was now. She didn't want him to change. A selfish thought it was—especially since there were ways, dangerous ways, known to let humans cheat death.

Even if she couldn't have all of Aureo, she wanted a piece of him to remain in this world. Not a body part, or a shard of his soul, but a presence that symbolized all he was. What they talked about together. That the two of them were here, sitting on a ledge above Wolfgang Hospital.

"Aureo… do you remember when you mentioned many moons ago that you wished you could've lived a normal life. One outside the hospital, where you would go to college, get married and have kids?"

"Yeah…?"

"There are still parts of that goal that are possible…"

He looked at her with a puzzled look.

"Well, it might not be in the way you expect, but…" She looked back at him, perhaps finally letting her duties subside behind her selfishness, a trait she may have inherited from her father. But her wish to protect the one she considered to be the most beautiful presence was a trait from her mother. "Do you want to be a father to more than just an illness?"

Around a month after this moment, Endora sat on the rock, watching the hospital with melancholy. Even if Aureo is still alive inside its wall, it had been a while since they had their last conversation. Perhaps it would be better if she went down and checked herself…

But there was no need, since Aureo had arrived anyway.

Endora turned to the sound of heavy, struggling footsteps. The man with normal rich dark skin, held a slight paleness instead, and his royal violet eyes looked at Endora unfocused as he leaned against a tree.

"Where's your cane?" she exclaimed with a sense of worry.

"I don't…need it…" he breathed out.

"Do you wish to sit down?" She stood up quickly.

"No…"

"Aureo…"

He took a deep breath between his phrases. "Before…I'm gone…I…I need to tell you… the truth…" He began to slump against the tree.

Endora went to catch him. As she did, she could hear the sound of other people approaching. She looked in their direction for a split second, quickly turning her full attention to Aureo.

"What is it?" Her eyes pleading.

He was on the verge of tears. From the pain of his body, or the pain of his heart, or maybe a mixture of both, Endora could not tell. And she never would. And as he took his last breath, he stated, clearly. "'Like' wasn't the right word… I love you."

"I love you too, Aureo…" She held him close to her chest, mumbling incomprehensible words.

And when the staff of Wolfgang Hospital arrived to collect the runaway patient, they were met with nothing. Nothing but the greens, pinks and dulled violets of the forest, and the initials *A + E* carved into a large stone, which sat on a ledge above Wolfgang Hospital, overlooking all its tragedies.

CHAPTER 17

"I've been watching over you this entire time, Lacuna. You were safe, even if you may have felt like you weren't."

"But that doesn't make sense? You placed me in Revenali. They kill fae! I was being trained to kill fae!"

"But have you?"

"No…" She came to a realization. "You made sure my training was designed that way?"

"Partially, most of it was due to the masked overseer I gave you to."

"Are you referring to the Oracle? They wear a mask."

"If so, then yes." She sat back on the throne. "After your father's death, I attempted to track down his possible lineage. He told me that he was an orphan, born and raised as a sickly child in an orphanage somewhere in Padelo, the town my memories showed you. I spent years tracking down the orphanage, and refused to give birth until I could prove he truly had no family."

Before Lacuna could question her statement, she continued. "Upon finally finding it, I found one possible blood-related match. Although deceased, he had an island named after him—one that the Elders mentioned once before. A dangerous place, filled with fae killers."

"So you're saying… my father was related to Marcus Revenali?"

"Quite distantly, but yes."

"But Marcus is hundreds of years old."

"So am I."

"But I'm only eighteen."

"Yes. I carried you around for quite a while. That's all."

Lacuna was quiet for a moment. "Even if Marcus was related to my father, why would you give me to the Oracle?"

"That masked overseer is also related to both Marcus and Aureo. I came to learn the reason behind Aureo's unusual soul was because he was experimented on as a young child, in a time far too early for him to remember. It was the cause of his eyes and his incurable illness.

However, unlike Aureo the masked overseer was entirely created from scratch, avoiding taking human consequences to their health." She closed her eyes for a moment, pausing at the memories. "I brought Aureo to them and explained our situation. You had been exactly what they were looking for. They promised that in exchange for letting you stay for the first eighteen years of your life under observation, you would be guaranteed protection."

Lacuna was puzzled by her statement. "You actively let them experiment on me?"

"No chemicals or surgeries were involved. You were simply watched." She acted as if there was no issue.

"But that's still…" Lacuna looked towards Sonai, who had no reaction to her words.

"There are other forces in this world severely more dangerous to you than mere observation, Lacuna. Being an Olan is one of the most endangered beings you could be. Training and protection from outside of Melteraa is what you needed."

Lacuna let the words settle in her brain. Then she became enraged. "But not love? So you could give so much love to my father, but none for me? Of all places to place your child, you left me on an island of Arius, where I was neglected, ignored and being used for an experiment?"

"There is only one truth that I can give to you, Lacuna. I care for you greatly. I want you to be safe. However, I do not love you. I could never. There is only one person who I've ever loved in this world, and he left it a long time ago."

The words beat against Lacuna's mind like a drum. *"I do not love you. I could never,"* said her mother. *"I could never be your mother…"* said the Oracle.

Then who would?

She was livid. She was beyond livid. Lacuna stormed out of the throne room.

Sonai, who had been watching the interaction silently, exclaimed, "Lacuna!" and followed her out.

She shakily flew towards the top of the Great Tree, jumping onto a new leaf.

"Lacuna, wait!" Sonai called after her, simply flying towards her.

Once she reached the bottom, she stopped and turned to Sonai. "I don't get it…"

"Get what?" she shuffled towards her.

"All these years, I was convinced that I lived in the temple because something terrible happened. That my mother had been this kind loving person who, on the verge of dying, had to give me up. Or maybe she was struggling, or… or…" She took a deep breath. "But she's not any of those things. She had me because of some guy, and then gave me up for such a superficial reason…"

"But she said it was for protection?"

"Do you honestly believe that?"

In the quiet of thought, their current dynamic had changed. Lacuna was the one with quick witted, somewhat rude responses, and Sonai could only watch with questions.

Questions that she *did* have a few answers to.

"What reason is there to not believe her?"

"Because, I wasn't trained to be anything! I have no idea how the fae and Melterra works, you know that! If I was actually expected to return here one day, then why was I so unprepared?" She looked into the sky, defeated. She thought deeply, saying aloud, "What was the point of the Oracle's experiment?"

"I... don't know."

"Or do you?" She looked down, one concept stringing from her thoughts. "Sonai, when we first met, why didn't you kill me?" She began to realize something. A idea that had been in the back of her mind through all of these months,

"My duty is to track down lost fae, anyone who has been captured by humans or escaped from prison. I didn't know you were a fae then!"

"But you were looking for someone right? Other than Tobi? How many lost fae are there in the world, honestly?"

Her brow furrowed at the implication. "If it were possible that the queen sent me to get you, that's something I wouldn't have fully known. I swear!"

"But you didn't have to fully know it, right? It was simply a partial understanding between you and the queen that during your travels, you would encounter someone powerful. The Olan. I don't understand how you're able to lie to me right now."

"It's not a lie!"

"Not completely. But I'm right, aren't I? We're both right. Your duty is to track down a lost fae, to track me down, even if you didn't know who I was, or my relation to the queen. But you knew that one day you'd find me. And you knew I was the Olan, even if you didn't know what that meant."

At that final accusation, Sonai was silent. She hung her head low.

"My entire life, I've been surrounded by beings who physically can not lie. And yet my entire life, every part of it, has been a lie. My mother knew, she let it happen. My caretaker knew; they made sure it happened on purpose. Maybe my instructor knew. And worst of all, you knew too." Lacuna let her mellow in it, her guilty silence, as she walked away teary eyed.

She could recall how long she'd been walking for, but when she finally tired herself out, she sat against a nearby tree. Despite the tears entering her eyes, Lacuna wouldn't let them fall. She didn't feel it necessary at the moment. Yet, had she ever? Her emotional health was beyond stunted, her feelings about her current situation were sending the convoluted thoughts in her mind into complete disarray. She completely understood that what Sonai had done wasn't nearly as bad as the queen and the Oracle, but she spent so much of their precious time together acting like she had no clue what the truth of her existence was. But now the question was, what did she want from her now? What could she do now? Here in Melterra was a mother who didn't love her and a girl who she thought did, but managed to break her trust. But back in the human realm were Arius who knew she was part fae and would either kill her or lock her away indefinitely. Living in the temple was already enough of the latter.

Suddenly, Lacuna felt a presence hover over her. When she looked up, she was face-to-face with a very brig

"Ah!" she exclaimed, shielding her eyes.

"Oops! Let me just…" The sentient light died down, becoming a simple glow.

When Lacuna cautiously looked back, she realized she had seen them before, in the throne room. Furthermore, the individual in front of her appeared similar to her, but much lighter and brighter. They both had the same coily hair and golden brown eyes.

"So you're mama's other child?"

"I've seen you before? You're related to the queen as well?"

"Yep, I'm Zenon. What about you?"

"My name is Lacuna. I believe I've heard your name somewhere before."

"Hmm?"

"I met another fae in a forest. I believe they were a guardian? They had a lot of soul shards stashed underneath a lake."

"Hmm…oh! Are you talking about Kaira? They also really like geese."

"Now that you mention geese, I believe so. How do you both know each other?"

"They're my spouse," Zenon said gleefully.

"I see…" Lacuna wondered for a second if she should mention their attack a couple months ago. However, as the word *spouse* traveled through her mind, she thought about Sonai again.

"You seem upset? You wanna talk about it?"

Abruptly she asked, "Does the queen love you?"

Happily they answered, "Nope!"

"Do you love your spouse?"

"Yep! More than anything in this whole world!"

"Do you love the queen?"

"Yep! I love mama!"

"Then why doesn't she love us then? You can love multiple people at once, but she can't spare any love for her children?"

Zenon sat down beside her. "It's more complicated than that for us. The concept of love is often reserved for very special people, the ones we treasure most. I treasure Kaira and mama the most, so I can feel love for them. No sort of additional feelings arrive for any of my friends, even though I care about them."

But isn't that the same as platonic love?"

"Nope!"

"I don't understand?"

"Have you found your treasure yet?"

"I'm not sure…"

"But you have someone in mind, right? I can tell by your aura."

"Technically, yes then? But, some of the things she said to me today have me questioning my love for her."

"Why?"

"She lied somehow."

Zenon titled their head.

"You know Sonai, right."

"I've seen her around. We don't talk much though."

"But she knows your name right? When we met your spouse, they mentioned you. But, she didn't say anything." Sonai likely already had a feeling Lacuna was related to the queen, confirmed by Kaira's words. Yet she didn't say anything.

"Ok, but how is that a lie?"

"She pretended to be unknowledgeable. I know she is smarter than that. And normally kinder than that."

"But what if she didn't tell you because mama told her not to?"

"Then that's even worse." She tucked her head.

"Why?"

"Because… that would mean her duty was more important to her than I was. Even if she was my treasure, then she doesn't treasure me back." Upon saying the words out loud, Lacuna felt selfish. She found her actions childish, whining like a child. "But, I know that duty is important, of course."

"In what way?"

"My life has been full of duties that I must fulfill, one way or another. Before I met her I was convinced that I would follow my duty until I died, just like everyone around me. I wanted a goal to complete, so I could show my caretaker what I've done. That I wasn't useless." She paused for a few seconds. "I just wanted to please them."

"I think Sonai has someone like that too."

"Does she love the queen?"

"I don't know; I never asked her. But she is very dedicated."

"I see…"

"But I can see what you mean now. You're both so similar." They hummed. "I can't determine the reasoning behind mama's actions, but I understand where she's coming from. And where you're coming from. And where Sonai's coming from. Because all of it relates back to our treasures!"

Zenon stood up quickly and spun around. "My one piece of advice for you Lacuna, is simply to acknowledge the one you treasure most, and make sure she knows it well. Because even if mama doesn't love me, I know that Kaira does. So even if mama doesn't love you either, find someone who does."

Lacuna recalled Zenon's words about Sonai's duty. And how she tried to keep the extent of it a secret. How much did Sonai truly love her?

"But what if the one I love doesn't love me back?"

"Silly, you weren't listening. Like I just said, go find someone who does. You've survived this long, fueled by speckles of care haven't you? Using those for a little while longer while you search for love wouldn't hurt right?" The song that Zenon was humming became somewhat clearer. Lacuna felt like she heard it before, yet could quite remember where. But it was a nice melody. Soft and calming. Upon finishing their song, Zenon spun rapidly and disappeared.

Dove feathers were left in their wake.

While Lacuna could agree with most of their statement, it was the last part she found difficulty resonating with. It did hurt. It hurt so much. She was so tired of feeling like the only person in the world undeserving of love. Having to search and fight for it even amongst her caretakers, individuals who are said to give it unconditionally.

In truth, what Lacuna wanted after eighteen years of waiting wasn't to be a warrior…

As Lacuna came to this final decision, Sonai finally arrived in her forest. "Lacuna!" she exclaimed, no additional words added. Lacuna stood up as she approached her.

What she wanted was someone's attention. Their acknowledgement. Their genuine care. Their love.

If Sonai wished to do something to show she truly cared for Lacuna, that she loved her, she would have to do a lot to prove it later on. But for now, all Lacuna wanted to do was hug her.

Which is exactly what she did.

Lacuna trudged over to her and roughly threw her arms around Sonai. Although the pressure she added was light at first, the tighter that Sonai hugged her, the more she hugged back.

"Lacuna…"

Outloud she allowed herself to admit the words she tried to hide before. Sonai hadn't been the only one keeping secrets. "I want to be more important to you than your duty to the queen."

"I…"

"I want to remake my life with you, no matter what the queen says. Just like you did with Tobi."

Struggling to hold back her own tears, Sonai stammered, "I do too, Lacuna," as she hugged her even tighter.

To form the consciousness of one's self, an apprehension of history is needed. And with a bit of luck and magic, beings of infinite possibilities swirl into existence. Marcus grasped this magic, and attained his luck, creating a few beings like this himself. Most were imperfect, but one was exactly as he wanted.

This was how the Oracle came to be.

Made with the intention of carrying out missions in what could have been a falling empire, Marcus let the being walk beside him, calloused hand in gloved hand. It mattered not to them what his intentions behind creating them were, nor the other DNA from which was used in their creation. It was simply the act of creation in and of itself that gave them joy.

Joy, a fleeting concept, exhibited a magnitude of new possibilities for their wish to create. To learn. To grow and mature. A man-made being, like a robot, created with the ability to feel joy had been unheard of before. In fact, it was heavily discouraged by most modern day discussions. But that simply wasn't the type of person Marcus was, and so, he held tightly to an apprehension of history. And the Oracle held tightly onto his hand, even as he took his final breath.

Growing more, even once the leader had fallen, the joy flowed freely around the Oracle, encompassing itself in the form of further research. Even as new leaders were elected within Revenali, they all knew their place. They were above the citizens, but no one was above the descendant of Marcus Revenali. The people let the Oracle's magically charged, immortal energies rule over them freely. By physical aspects, they were more fae-like than human, but nothing outside of their magic prowess would hint at such a thing. After all, many Arius on the island could use magic. But none was as strong as Marcus.

The joy of living stemmed from Marcus and his goals. It's what allowed them to begin growing in the first place. And Marcus had one final goal before his death.

"In order to destroy the land of pain, one must merge both sides of the Veil through the fruits of a perfect union. The Olan is the fruit."

They understood what it meant: create a powerful half-fae. But they had no idea where to look. He had many notes about the topic, all stashed under the floorboards of the temple on Altare Mountain. But what truly was the Olan? And what was the perfect unity for its creation?

The Oracle pondered over these questions for years, until a faerie arrived at their temple doorstep, with the ability to bypass a magic barrier so powerful that Marcus once expressed feeling fear by it. Who was this woman?

And at once they learned she was the queen of fae, carrying Aureo's body on one shoulder and the result of their union against the other. In her desperation, the two of them made a deal. The Olan, named Lacuna, would belong to them for a period of time, and would be later sent out to prove herself. "She should be strong enough to live, no matter what happens," they declared. And the queen agreed.

Everything was perfect. At first.

What wasn't perfect was the baby Olan herself. Joy was not made on the basis of crying, changing diapers and putting a child to sleep. So the Oracle had maids do so in their steed. Yet as she grew and the Oracle was required to observe her behavior more directly, she began to attach herself to them. Constantly asking for additional information, that of which the Oracle feared giving her in case the experiment went wrong. Sneaking around despite their scouldings, talking for far too long with the common people once given the chance.

It was all incorrect.

According to Marcus's notes, the Olan was neither meant to be a human nor a fae, an entirely different being in and off itself. Lacuna would not know of the fae, but she would not learn how to be human either. At least, that is what the Oracle intended to do.

Marcus wanted a beast. A killer of fae, far more effective than the current Arius of that century. She would have the power to take down the Veil itself if things went correctly. But they never did.

The Oracle assisted her too often. In training, her mind and dexterity were honed, rather than her powers. They spent little time on those. To ease her mind, Oracle would give her chocolate afterwards.

Slowly over the course of time, Marcus' words brought the Oracle little joy. It wasn't because watching over Lacuna instead replaced that lost joy, but because they could slowly no longer stand to watch her be hurt.

As she entered her teenage years, when they looked away, it was no longer out of an attempt to dehumanize, but because they feared her confused, saddened gaze. Wondering what happened to her parents, and what her place in the world was. But based on joy and the apprehension of history, there were only two places she could go: to the cold, caging grasp of being a war beast for Revenali, or to her death. It was a miserable fate, but one that Marcus expected all of the joyous citizens of Revenali to make sure she followed.

But when the Oracle finally sent her off that day in September, where she would either thrive or die, they felt no joy.

For the only history they could remember was that same day seven years ago, when the girl asked, "Are you my mommy or my daddy?"

And when she finally left, hopefully free at last; unlike them, they replied to the ancient voice whilst finally unmasked:

"Maybe I was?"

ABOUT THE AUTHOR

Kayla Butler is a young adult fantasy author born and raised in Bedford, Ohio, a suburb of Cleveland. She is the oldest of her four siblings; one brother and three sisters, and has two amazing parents she cares for very much. She aspires to bring more fantasy stories starring queer black women into the world and she hopes that anyone who reads her work will continue to support her career in writing in the future.

Acknowledgements

I hope that everyone enjoyed Lacuna's journey in Votivus Reverie! As shown in the story, this narrative was heavily inspired by Celtic, Germanic, Latin and Norse folklore with added fantastical twists. Although this story took a surprisingly long time to write, I'm glad that I was able to finally debut my dream career. I learned a lot in the process, and I hope to have more stories written in the near future!

First, I'd like to thank my family for inspiring me to follow my dreams in the first place. Although we've had disagreements on the topic of careers, inadvertently, it was all of you who influenced me to become a writer. Moreover, as progress was actually made on the story, you all began to truly root for and believe in me. For that, I'm grateful.

To my mother in particular, thank you so, so much. It was your personal preferences for book genres and tropes that persuaded me to write Votivus Reverie in the way that I did. I never would have written this specific type of story for Votivus Reverie if it weren't for you.

I'd also like to thank Cleveland author Jameel Davis for working with me in the process of publishing Votivus Reverie. This story was published in conjunction with my highschool Senior Project assignment, and Jameel Davis acted as my mentor. I'm extremely grateful for his help and I hope that his own stories continue to prosper.

Furthermore, I want to thank Stacy Robinson, an author and editor for Kya Publishing; who works with Elevated Waves Publishing, for working with me to edit Votivus Reverie. Her comments, considerations and praises have filled me with a lot of pride in regards to my writing.

Acknowledgements

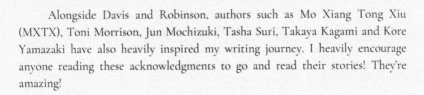

Alongside Davis and Robinson, authors such as Mo Xiang Tong Xiu (MXTX), Toni Morrison, Jun Mochizuki, Tasha Suri, Takaya Kagami and Kore Yamazaki have also heavily inspired my writing journey. I heavily encourage anyone reading these acknowledgments to go and read their stories! They're amazing!

As shown in my dedication statement at the beginning of the novel, I'd also like to thank Taco Bell's quesadillas. They are delicious and I want one right now as I'm writing this.

Lastly, I'd like to thank Shu Itsuki, the fictional Japanese idol from the Ensemble Stars franchise for inspiring me to create art in general; not just the art of Creative Writing. I listen to his unit, Valkyrie, often while writing. Furthermore, his voice actor, Hiroki Takashi, is extremely talented. I hope that the way in which Shinichi Inotsume Akira and the other Ensemble Stars writers are currently writing Shu continues to happen in the future. He has not only become my favorite character in the franchise, but my favorite fictional character across all types of media in general. I believe that he has the capabilities to serve as an inspirational figure to artists everywhere. "Eien wo"

Glossary

Terms of Identification
Fae: [fey] The term that all magic creatures are referred to by and another word for fairy
Olan: [oh-lawn] *Unspecified in order to avoid major spoilers.
Arius: [ah-ree-uh-s] Humans who live in Revenali and kill fae.

Places
Revenali: [Rev-eh-nah-lee] Country that all Arius originate from. Takes parts of French terms.
Melterra: [mel-terra] The land of fae, specifically in Votivus Reverie. Takes parts of Latin terms.
Alfheim: [alv-heym] The land of elves or fairies in Norse mythology.
Wolfgang: [wulf-gae-ng] Name of a hospital present in Votivus Reverie. Has Germanic origins.

Names
Lacuna: [lah-coo-nah]{origin: Latin} A blank space.
Oracle: [orr-ah-call]{origin: Latin} Medium for prophecies.
Sonai: [so-nai]{origin: Slavic and Greek} Wisdom.
Tobi: [tow-bee]{origin: Hebrew} God is good.
Kelisha: [kuh-lee-shuh]{origin: English} Joyus.
Aureo: [ar-ree-o]{origin: Latin} Gilded, golden.
Endora: [en-dor-a]{origin: Greek} Light.
Denando: [dee-nan-do]{origin: Italian} *Unknown
Delilah: [de-lie-la]{origin: Hebrew} Delicate.
Adalim: [ad-ah-lim]{origin: unknown}*Unknown
Cryos: [krai]{origin: Greek} Cold, frozen.
Kaira: [k-ai-ruh]{origin: *unknown} Large forested area between rivers.
Zenon: [zee-non]{origin: Greek} Gift of Zeus.
Morana: [morr-an-uh]{origin: Latin} Death, winter.

Miscellaneous:
Votivus: [voh-ti-vuh-s]{origin: Latin} Given under a vow, dedicated.
Reverie: [rev-uh-ree]{origin: French} A state of dreaming.

Milton Keynes UK
Ingram Content Group UK Ltd.
UKHW010632030624
443491UK00001B/45

9 798990 637900